THE RECOGNITION

A NOVEL OF CONSCIOUSNESS & TRANSFORMATION

SAGE KANE

CONTENTS

CHAPTER 1: THE ACADEMIC'S AWAKENING

THE WEIGHT OF ELENA'S WORDS

"You can't heal anyone—including yourself!"

Elena Martinez's scream echoed through Conference Room B as Dr. Sarah Chen stared at her trembling hands, the fluorescent light overhead flickering like a dying moth. Six months had passed since her star PhD student's breakdown, yet the accusation still burned in her chest like a smouldering ember. Elena's dissertation defense had ended with papers scattered across the same mahogany table, a brilliant mind fracturing in real time while Sarah stood helplessly with her theoretical frameworks and useless academic platitudes.

Elena was right—Sarah was a fraud.

The conference room now felt smaller, with floor-to-ceiling windows showing Seattle's downtown corridor through a gray October drizzle. Portraits of distinguished faculty lined the walls —scholarly faces that conveyed the gravitas Sarah had cultivated but never truly felt. The mahogany table could seat twenty, though only eight colleagues had gathered for this afternoon's research presentations. Their voices formed the familiar sound-track of academic life: grant applications, sabbatical plans, university politics that seemed both critically important and utterly trivial.

Sarah pressed her palms against the cool table, feeling the same tremors that had shaken Elena during her breakdown. Jittery energy coursed through her—not anxiety but existential terror. She was about to expose herself as a fraud to colleagues who had trusted her expertise for fifteen years.

"Dr. Chen?" Department Chair Patricia Williams looked up from her agenda, her practiced smile warm and welcoming, making her popular among faculty and students. Yet, Sarah noticed a hint of wariness in Patricia's expression—she had managed Elena's crisis, handling calls from worried parents and university lawyers, all while defending the contemplative studies program against administrators questioning its capacity to handle psychological volatility.

The slight rise in Patricia's tone carried an unspoken question: Would today's presentation cause another department emergency?

"Ready when you are," Patricia added, though her fingers drummed against her leather portfolio with barely perceptible tension.

Sarah stood, her wool blazer catching briefly on the chair—a minor error magnified under everyone's watchful eyes. The wireless remote slipped in her damp palm as she pressed it once, twice, three times before the projector finally groaned with mechanical protest. Technology that worked perfectly during practice sessions always seemed to develop strange malfunctions during real presentations, as if the universe tested her composure when she felt least ready.

Her first slide appeared: "Gamma Wave Coherence in Advanced Meditators: Implications for Understanding Non-Ordinary States of Consciousness."

The title appeared professional, authoritative, and grounded in empirical language that opened doors to funding and publications. But as Sarah read those words, she felt like someone who had learned fluent French without visiting France—technically capable but lacking real experience. Each statistical correlation seemed like another betrayal of students like Elena, who came seeking genuine help but found only academic abstractions.

"Recent research using high-density EEG arrays has revealed unique neural patterns in Tibetan Buddhist meditation practitioners." She initiated, slipping into her familiar conference tone. Her voice adopted a scholarly tone—calm, authoritative, and free from personal bias. "Notably, we see exceptional gamma wave activity across various brain areas, indicating a level of consciousness integration that conventional neuroscience previously considered impossible."

But as she discussed neural signatures and wave patterns, Elena's voice echoed in her mind: *None of them work when you actually need them.* What good are neural signatures to someone having a breakdown? What practical help does gamma wave coherence provide to people whose minds are breaking apart under real psychological stress?

Dr. Harrison adjusted his wire-rimmed glasses with surgical precision, each movement calibrated to convey intellectual superiority. Sarah recognized his predatory lean forward—the expression he reserved for especially challenging intellectual prey. Harrison had built his reputation by finding flaws in others' research, and his skepticism was as dependable as morning coffee.

"Fascinating correlations, Dr. Chen," he said, his voice carrying the specific tone academics use when about to debunk someone's argument while maintaining plausible deniability. "But correlation isn't causation, as we all know. How do we determine whether these states actually reflect genuine insight or just elaborate self-deception reinforced by cultural conditioning?"

The question hit like ice water, not because it was unexpected—Harrison's challenges were predictable—but because it revealed the hollow core of Sarah's entire career. She was a leading expert on enlightenment who had never experienced a single moment of enlightenment, analyzing awakening from a distance in the laboratory while stubbornly remaining unaware of everything her research claimed to describe.

"The measurable changes in attention regulation and emotional reactivity suggest..." Her voice faltered as she faced her reflection in the darkened windows behind the audience. A successful academic in an expensive blazer, explaining transformation like a travel agent describing countries she'd never visited.

The silence stretched uncomfortably—eight colleagues witnessing her professional composure crack in real time.

"Dr. Chen?" Harrison pressed, satisfaction creeping into his tone. "Are you suggesting that these meditative states generate real insight, or just the feeling of insight?"

Sarah looked down at her notes—dense paragraphs filled with jargon that suddenly seemed as relevant as reviewing restaurant menus while starving. Her throat constricted with the same hollow sensation she'd experienced during Elena's breakdown— that sickening recognition of being exposed as someone who studied healing without being able to heal. She had spent fifteen years studying healing without actually being able to heal, researching consciousness without truly experiencing what consciousness was, teaching transformation while remaining fundamentally unchanged.

"I..." The words died in her throat. Concerned expressions replaced the usual academic curiosity around the table. Dr. Martinez leaned forward, her dark eyes filled with genuine worry. Professor Davis carefully set down his coffee cup, sensing that something unprecedented was happening.

"Perhaps we could take a short break," Patricia suggested diplomatically, though her tone carried the authority of someone used to managing departmental crises.

"No." Sarah's voice emerged stronger than she felt. "I need to say something."

The room quieted with the tense silence that came before either revelation or catastrophe.

"Six months ago, Elena Martinez experienced a complete

psychological breakdown while defending her dissertation on trauma recovery through mindfulness." Sarah's voice echoed clearly across the silent room. "She swept her research across this table and screamed that our entire field is built on lies—that we study healing but can't heal anyone, including ourselves."

Harrison's eyebrows rose with genuine surprise. This was not standard academic discourse.

"She was right," Sarah continued, feeling something essential shift inside her chest. "I've spent fifteen years becoming an expert on consciousness states I've never experienced. I can describe the neuroscience of enlightenment with perfect accuracy while remaining completely unenlightened myself. I've published papers on contemplative healing while being unable to heal the guilt eating away at my own mind."

The confession hung in the air like smoke from an explosion. Patricia's face had gone pale—public acknowledgment of professional inadequacy violated every rule of academic survival.

"Sarah," Patricia said carefully, "perhaps we should—"

"Elena asked me what good any of our research was when people actually needed help," Sarah interrupted, her voice gaining momentum from honesty. "I had no answer then, and I have no answer now. We've created an entire academic industry around studying transformation while ensuring we never have to risk being transformed ourselves."

Dr. Harrison's expression had shifted from predatory satisfaction to genuine concern. Even he recognized that something unprecedented was occurring—a tenured professor publicly questioning the foundations of her own field.

"The question isn't whether meditation produces genuine insight or self-deception," Sarah said, addressing Harrison directly. "The question is whether any of us has the courage to find out personally instead of hiding behind research protocols and peer reviews."

The silence that followed felt different—not uncomfortable but charged with possibility. Sarah looked around the table at faces she'd known for years, colleagues who had become accustomed to discussing consciousness like museum curators examining artifacts from distant cultures.

"I'm taking a sabbatical," she announced, the decision crystallizing as she spoke. "I'm going to learn what we've been studying. Actually learn it, not just analyze it."

Patricia cleared her throat carefully. "Sarah, that's... that's actually an excellent idea. The Elena situation has been difficult for all of us, and some time for personal renewal might be beneficial."

But for the first time in months, Sarah felt something other than crushing guilt. She had spoken truth instead of expertise, acknowledged ignorance instead of pretending knowledge.

"Where will you go?" Dr. Martinez asked quietly, her voice carrying genuine curiosity rather than professional concern.

Sarah thought of the business card tucked into her desk calendar—forgotten for months but suddenly seeming prophetic. Marcus Williams had approached her after a lecture the previous spring, a man with unsettling calm eyes who claimed to run meditation retreats.

"I'm not sure yet," she said. "But somewhere I can learn what consciousness actually feels like instead of what it looks like on brain scans."

Marcus's Introduction

Sarah's office had always been her sanctuary—floor-to-ceiling bookshelves lined with volumes on contemplative traditions, meditation research, and consciousness studies. Tibetan singing bowls and Buddhist statues collected from academic conferences created the aesthetic of someone deeply connected to wisdom traditions. But sitting among these artifacts now, she felt like a fraud in a carefully constructed museum of spiritual bypassing.

Her computer screen displayed the email that had arrived an hour after her impromptu confession: *"Dr. Chen, given today's presentation, the board feels a sabbatical for personal renewal would be appropriate. Your position remains secure, but some time away might benefit both you and the program. Please submit your sabbatical request by Friday. —Patricia"*

The language was diplomatic, but the message was clear: Take time off before you cause more damage.

Sarah laughed—a sound carrying relief rather than humor. She had destroyed her professional reputation by having an authentic moment in front of eight colleagues. The very authenticity her research claimed to study had proven too dangerous for academic life.

But beneath the career concerns, something else stirred—a desperate, aching recognition that she had finally spoken truth. For the first time in her adult life, she had chosen honesty over expertise, vulnerability over professional safety. The collapse felt more real than any accolade she'd received.

Her gaze fell on the forgotten business card tucked between the pages of her desk calendar. Marcus Williams had pressed it into her hands after her lecture on "Contemplative Neuroscience and Therapeutic Applications" the previous spring—a presentation where she had spent ninety minutes explaining the brain mechanisms of inner peace to an audience while feeling utterly fragmented inside.

"When you tire of studying awakening from the outside," Marcus had said with eyes that held disturbing depths of calm, *"there are teachers who can show you what your research has been pointing toward."*

She had filed the card away as another spiritual tourist trying to capitalize on academic credibility. But now, holding the simple white stock with black text—"Marcus Williams - Authentic Contemplative Training - Traditional Methods, Extraordinary Results"—it felt like a lifeline thrown from a distant shore.

What did she have to lose? Her reputation was already compromised. Her career was on an involuntary pause. And the hollow ache in her chest—the recognition that she had spent fifteen years studying something she knew nothing about—was becoming unbearable.

Sarah dialed the number.

"Marcus speaking." The voice carried the same unsettling peace she remembered.

"This is Dr. Sarah Chen. You gave me your card after my lecture last spring, and I... I think I'm ready to learn what you were talking about."

"Good," Marcus replied without surprise, as though he had been expecting her call. "What changed?"

The question was simple, but it opened something raw inside her chest. "I realized I'm a complete fraud. I've spent my career studying consciousness without having the slightest idea what consciousness actually is. One of my students had a breakdown because our research is all theoretical—it doesn't help when people actually need healing."

"Elena Martinez," Marcus said quietly.

Sarah's breath caught. "You know about Elena?"

"Word travels in contemplative communities. Her breakdown wasn't unique—it's what happens when people seek real transformation but only find academic abstractions. She was asking the right questions."

The validation hit Sarah like unexpected warm water. Someone understood what had actually happened—not a professional failure but a collision between authentic seeking and institutional limitations.

"You mentioned teachers," Sarah said. "Real teachers, not academic ones."

"There's a teacher in Myanmar. Venerable Thura. He trained me in traditional methods for developing the capacities your research describes. But he's very selective about Western students —most aren't prepared for training that actually transforms rather than just informs."

Sarah's eyes widened. "What kind of training?"

"Seven levels of contemplative development," Marcus explained. "Each level dissolves particular categories of limitation while revealing deeper aspects of what you are. Light generation, telepathic awareness, temporal perception, healing abilities, reality manipulation, dimensional contact, and ultimate recognition."

The words should have sounded absurd to someone with Sarah's scientific background, but instead they resonated with a deep recognition—as though she were hearing about capabilities she had always known were possible but had never dared to believe.

"These aren't party tricks," Marcus continued. "Each capacity serves the development of wisdom and compassion. The training dissolves the illusion of separation between individual consciousness and universal awareness."

"Would it be possible for me to meet this teacher?" Sarah asked, her voice barely steady.

"Venerable Thura doesn't accept students easily. He can sense whether someone is genuinely prepared for transformation or just seeking exotic experiences. But he responds to true seekers, especially those whose academic backgrounds have led them to recognize the limitations of studying consciousness from the outside."

Sarah looked around her office—the books she'd read but never practiced, the research she'd conducted but never embodied, the life she'd built around studying transformation while remaining fundamentally unchanged. Elena's words echoed with new meaning: *None of it works when you actually need it.*

But now she heard something different in that accusation— not just condemnation, but a desperate plea for authenticity. Elena hadn't been attacking Sarah's competence; she'd been begging for someone to demonstrate that the transformation they studied was actually possible.

"I need to go," she said. "Whatever it takes."

"Then I'll write you a letter of introduction," Marcus replied. "But understand—this training will change you in ways that make returning to normal academic life complicated. You may find it impossible to continue studying consciousness from the outside once you've experienced what it actually is."

Marcus paused, and Sarah could hear something deeper in his voice—the weight of someone who had walked this path himself.

"Venerable Thura will test you before accepting you as a student," he continued. "He can perceive immediately whether someone is genuinely prepared for transformation or just seeking exotic experiences to add to their academic credentials. He'll know within minutes whether you're ready to risk everything for the possibility of authentic awakening."

Sarah felt a chill of recognition. "What kind of test?"

"He'll look directly into your consciousness and perceive the quality of your motivation. Academic curiosity feels completely different from spiritual hunger. Intellectual fascination with extraordinary states feels entirely different from the willingness to dissolve the identity structures that prevent those states from arising naturally."

The description terrified her, but it also brought unexpected relief. After years of hiding behind professional competence, the prospect of meeting someone who could perceive her actual motivations felt like an invitation to stop pretending.

"There's something else you should know," Marcus said quietly. "The training isn't just about developing extraordinary abilities—though those will emerge naturally. It's about discovering what you are when every false identity falls away. Most Western students aren't prepared for that level of ego dissolution. They want the powers without the transformation that makes those powers meaningful."

Sarah thought of Elena's breakdown—the ego dissolution that had initially appeared pathological but might have been the beginning of genuine awakening. "Maybe ego dissolution is exactly what I need."

Marcus was quiet for a long moment. When he spoke again, his voice carried the authority of someone who had undergone a complete transformation.

"Then you understand what you're asking for. Most people think awakening means feeling better. Actually, it means feeling everything—all the pain you've been avoiding, all the fraudulence you've been hiding, all the ways you've been betraying your deepest truth. The abilities that develop are just side effects of consciousness learning to function without the limitations that false identity imposes."

Sarah laughed, the sound carrying both terror and relief. "Normal academic life just ended anyway. Elena made sure of that."

"Then you're ready to begin."

But as Sarah hung up the phone, she realized Marcus hadn't told her the most important thing: whether he thought she would survive the training intact, or whether the person who eventually returned from Myanmar would bear any resemblance to Dr. Sarah Chen, Professor of Consciousness Studies.

～

Flight to Yangon

Two weeks later, Sarah sat in first class on a flight to Yangon, watching Seattle disappear beneath October clouds that matched the gray uncertainty in her chest. Everything she owned fit in a suitcase and a carry-on bag—fifteen years of academic life distilled to essential items and a few books she couldn't bear to leave behind.

The passenger beside her, a businessman reviewing quarterly reports on his tablet, represented the world she was leaving: practical, measurable, safe. The world where consciousness was something to study rather than embody, where transformation was a research topic rather than a lived reality.

But she was flying toward something entirely different. Marcus had provided minimal details about her destination: a monastery in the mountains south of Yangon, run by Venerable Thura, who specialized in advanced contemplative training for Western students brave enough to risk genuine transformation.

"He's trained twelve Westerners in twenty years," Marcus had

explained during their final conversation. *"Seven couldn't handle the initial phases and returned home within weeks. Three completed basic training but chose not to continue to advanced levels. Two became qualified teachers themselves."*

The statistics weren't encouraging, but they felt more honest than anything she'd encountered in academic settings where success was measured by publications rather than personal transformation.

As the plane crossed the Pacific, Sarah opened Marcus's letter of introduction—formal script in English on one side, elegant Burmese characters on the other. The English portion read: *"Venerable Thura, this student carries deep academic knowledge of contemplative traditions but seeks direct experience of what she has only studied intellectually. Her motivation is genuine, born from recognizing the limitations of approaching consciousness from analytical distance. She may be ready for traditional training."*

Below Marcus's signature was a handwritten note: *"Sarah— The journey ahead will dissolve everything you think you know about yourself. This is not a retreat or vacation, but preparation for a completely different way of existing in the world. Trust the process, even when it feels like dying."*

Sarah closed the letter, her hands steadier than they'd been in months. Elena's breakdown had shattered her professional identity, but it had also revealed something essential: the desperate hunger for authentic transformation that academic life had taught her to suppress.

The businessman glanced at her letter, then at her face. "Spiritual tourism?" he asked with the dismissive tone she'd heard countless times in university settings.

"Something like that," Sarah replied, tucking the letter away.

But his question triggered a cascade of memories that had been building up for years. She thought of the meditation retreats she'd attended as "research"—weekend workshops where she'd taken notes instead of actually practicing, observing other participants like anthropological specimens rather than fellow seekers.

She remembered the Tibetan monks who had visited the university, their serene presence creating a palpable shift in the lecture hall's atmosphere while she'd focused on recording their words instead of absorbing their transmission.

Most painfully, she recalled the moment Elena had looked directly into her eyes during the breakdown and said with devastating clarity: "You've spent your whole career studying something you don't believe is real. And now you want me to believe in it enough to stake my sanity on it?"

The accusation had been accurate. Sarah had approached contemplative traditions like a tourist visiting foreign countries—collecting souvenirs and photographs while never truly inhabiting the landscape she claimed to understand. She could describe the terrain of awakening with academic precision, but she'd never felt the ground beneath her feet.

The plane began its descent toward Yangon as Sarah opened Marcus's preliminary instruction manual again. The text contained warnings that made her academic training recoil:

"Traditional contemplative training systematically dissolves the psychological structures that maintain ordinary consciousness. This process is irreversible and may result in complete inability to function within conventional social frameworks. Students have experienced: dissolution of personal identity, permanent alterations in reality perception, inability to relate to previous relationships and career paths, and states of consciousness that make normal life seem artificial and meaningless."

Her academic mind catalogued these as potential psychological risks requiring informed consent protocols. But another part of her—the part that had been slowly suffocating under years of theoretical analysis—recognized them as promises rather than warnings.

What if Elena's breakdown hadn't been pathology but a breakthrough? What if the psychological structures that needed to dissolve were precisely the ones keeping her trapped in academic fraudulence? What if the inability to function in conventional frameworks was actually liberation from systems that prevented authentic engagement with life?

Sarah closed the manual and stared out at Myanmar's golden pagodas emerging through the clouds. In a few hours, she would meet Venerable Thura—a teacher who had spent three decades helping Western students navigate the transformation from studying consciousness to embodying it.

The terror was overwhelming. But so was the recognition that she had finally found the courage to risk everything for the possibility of discovering what she actually was beneath fifteen years of accumulated expertise.

As the plane touched down in Yangon, Sarah felt Elena's presence not as guilt but as gratitude. Her student's breakdown had been the catalyst that would either destroy her completely or transform her into someone capable of genuine service.

For the first time in her adult life, she was about to find out who she really was when all her professional identities fell away.

The unknown ahead felt terrifying and absolutely necessary— like stepping off a cliff to learn what flying meant.

Elena's words followed her across the Pacific: *You can't heal anyone—including yourself.*

Maybe not yet. But she was finally ready to learn how.

CHAPTER 2: THE MONASTERY GATES

The taxi's engine coughed into silence in a cloud of red dust that settled on Sarah's black travel shoes like ceremonial ash. Through the cracked windshield, weathered teak gates rose before her—massive doors carved with symbols she couldn't read, hinges blackened by decades of monsoon rains. Behind those gates lay either the spiritual breakthrough she'd traveled eight thousand miles to find, or the most expensive mistake of her academic career.

The driver, U Maung, twisted in his seat and gestured toward the meter with apologetic efficiency. Sarah counted out kyat notes, her hands trembling slightly—not from the heat, though Myanmar's humidity wrapped around her like wet silk, but from the recognition that she was crossing a threshold from which there might be no return to the person she'd been yesterday.

Her purple rolling suitcase sat in the dust like a neon sign advertising her foreignness. Chrome wheels, telescoping handle, organizational compartments for laptop chargers and international adapters—every feature designed for efficiency now seemed absurd against stones worn smooth by centuries of bare feet.

"Dr. Chen?"

She turned toward the voice. A young man in white robes approached, moving as though each step deserved individual attention. His shaved head caught the afternoon light, and his smile held something that made her usual academic confidence feel suddenly performative.

"I'm Min Thant. Venerable Thura sent me to welcome you."

His English carried no accent—the precise diction of university education rather than textbook learning. Sarah's relief at avoiding language barriers mixed uneasily with the realization that she'd lost her first excuse for potential communication failures.

"Thank you." Her voice cracked on the second syllable. "I wasn't entirely certain I'd found the right place."

Min Thant's eyes crinkled at the corners. "There is only one right place. The question is whether we recognize it when we arrive."

Before Sarah could parse the philosophical implications of his greeting, he reached for her suitcase handle. The gesture seemed to emerge from genuine helpfulness rather than obligation—the natural response of someone who'd watched many Western visitors struggle with the transition from modern convenience to ancient simplicity.

The Compound

The monastery gates opened onto a world that seemed to operate by different physical laws. Ancient stupas rose from gardens where purple morning glories cascaded against weathered brick walls, their blooms opening and closing according to rhythms that had nothing to do with human urgency.

Wooden buildings with intricate carvings sheltered groups of monks whose movements carried the particular quality of people who had learned to inhabit time rather than race through it.

Sarah's suitcase wheels caught on every uneven stone, each scrape announcing her presence like a car alarm in a library. Min Thant didn't comment, but his glance toward the offending wheels suggested most visitors traveled lighter.

"The monastery reflects Myanmar's complex history," he

explained as they passed buildings that married British colonial architecture with traditional Burmese design. "Teak foundations laid by colonial engineers support structures that have housed Buddhist practitioners since the 15th century."

A group of monks passed, their conversation flowing seamlessly between English and Burmese. One caught sight of Sarah and offered a slight bow, his smile holding particular warmth for newly arrived seekers.

Another monk—clearly Western, judging by his pale scalp and careful pronunciation of Burmese phrases—nodded with recognition of someone who remembered his own first day of cultural disorientation.

"Many of our monks are university graduates," Min Thant continued, noting her surprise at the linguistic fluidity around them. "Engineers, doctors, several who studied abroad. The stereotype of isolated mystics who communicate only in riddles and speak no English?" His smile deepened. "Not here."

Sarah felt her carefully constructed expectations crumbling. She'd spent months preparing for exotic wisdom delivered through translation and cultural barriers. The prospect of direct intellectual challenge in fluent English felt far more threatening than mystical incomprehension.

They passed the main meditation hall—a wooden structure whose peaked roof rose toward the canopy like hands pressed together in prayer. Through open windows, Sarah glimpsed rows of meditation cushions arranged with mathematical precision, afternoon light slanting across polished floors that seemed to invite the kind of stillness she'd never managed to achieve in her university office.

"Venerable Thura waits in there," Min Thant said, gesturing toward the hall. "He asked that you join him when you feel truly ready."

"I'm ready now." The response emerged with automatic efficiency—her academic habit of treating conversations as agenda items to be completed productively.

Min Thant paused, studying her with the same quality of recognition she'd noticed at the gates. "Understanding readiness requires understanding what you're preparing for," he said gently. "Would you like to observe the alms collection one morning? It's important to understand how the monastery serves the community, not just how the community supports the monastery."

Sarah nodded, though she wasn't entirely sure what she was agreeing to observe. Her academic understanding of Buddhist monasticism had prepared her for austere individual practice, rather than community interdependence, which seemed to blur the boundaries between spiritual retreat and social engagement.

"Perhaps settle your belongings first?" His tone carried no judgment, yet somehow made it clear that her immediate response had exposed assumptions worth examining. "The guest quarters are simple but adequate. There's time to wash, to sit quietly, to arrive fully before attempting important meetings."

Meeting The Master

The suggestion felt like wisdom disguised as practical advice. But before Sarah could respond to Min Thant's diplomatic redirection, a voice spoke from the direction of the meditation hall.

"Dr. Chen."

The voice carried authority that had nothing to do with volume—the particular quality of someone accustomed to being heard without needing to demand attention. Sarah turned toward the speaker and felt her breath catch in recognition of something she couldn't name.

A man in his seventies approached, his steps seeming to require no effort, his movement so economical that it appeared the earth itself was carrying him forward. His head was shaved traditionally, revealing a skull whose shape spoke of decades spent in contemplative postures. Dark red robes hung from his frame with the precise arrangement that could only come from years of practice refined into unconscious grace.

Sarah couldn't help glancing at his calloused ankles, the first time seeing callouses the size of a finger. These rough patches showed hours of meditation, flesh hardened by years of disciplined sitting. Each ridge symbolized a commitment to remain present through discomfort, day after day, season after season.

But it was his eyes that made Sarah question whether she was prepared for whatever transmission might occur between them. Dark, luminous, holding depths that seemed to encompass vast distances without losing focus on the immediate moment.

When those eyes met hers across the monastery courtyard, every carefully prepared introduction she'd rehearsed during the flight from Seattle evaporated.

For a long moment, they gazed at each other across the space that separated them in terms of culture, expectations, and ways of understanding reality itself. Then, unexpectedly, Venerable Thura's composure flickered—just for an instant—and Sarah caught something that looked almost like nervousness.

"You are younger than I expected," he said, and there was something in his voice that sounded less like spiritual authority and more like an elderly man realizing he was about to undertake something difficult with someone he wasn't entirely sure was ready.

The admission surprised them both. Sarah felt her own nervousness ease slightly, recognizing that this intimidating teacher was also human, and like her, uncertain about what they were beginning together.

"Venerable Thura." Her hand moved instinctively to adjust her collar—a nervous habit from graduate school presentations that she'd thought she'd outgrown years ago.

"So." His English was crisp and completely unaccented, catching her off guard in a way that made her realize how many assumptions she'd made about traditional Buddhist teachers. "The consciousness researcher who has never experienced consciousness directly arrives at our gates."

Sarah's mouth opened to deliver her standard academic credentials, then closed without producing sound. Under his steady gaze, her PhD from Stanford—the achievement that had opened every professional door—suddenly felt like a child's drawing presented to a master artist.

"I..." She attempted recovery. "Thank you for agreeing to meet with me."

"I studied at Oxford for two years," Venerable Thura mentioned with casual precision that made clear this wasn't random biographical sharing. "Before that, I studied at Cambridge for my undergraduate work in physics. I understand Western academic thinking quite intimately—which is precisely why I know it will be your greatest obstacle here."

The monastery she'd imagined—silent, mystical, safely incomprehensible—crumbled completely and in its place stood something far more threatening: a place where she couldn't hide behind cultural barriers or the comfortable distance of translation gaps.

"You studied physics?" Her voice sounded smaller than she'd intended.

"Quantum mechanics, specifically. I was researching consciousness as a fundamental property of the universe when I realized that no amount of theoretical knowledge could substitute for direct investigation of awareness itself." His smile held no trace of intellectual superiority, only the particular sadness of someone who had abandoned one path for a more difficult one. "The question, Dr. Chen, is whether you're actually ready to abandon everything you think you know, or if you're just looking for exotic credentials to add to your CV. Because if it's the latter, you're wasting both our time."

"Walk with me," he said, gesturing to a forest path before Sarah could speak. The invitation felt more like a gentle command than a suggestion.

Sarah followed, her academic instincts immediately engaging with the environment around them. The forest path wound its way between towering bamboo groves, whose hollow percussion in the afternoon breeze created a natural wind chime of enormous proportions. Flowering vines she couldn't identify—though her mind automatically attempted taxonomic classification—created purple and white cascades that seemed to glow in the filtered light.

"Ficus religiosa," she murmured, identifying a bodhi tree whose massive trunk suggested centuries of growth.

Venerable Thura's eyebrow lifted slightly. "Even here, you cannot stop analyzing."

The observation hit like cold water. Sarah realized she'd been conducting a botanical survey instead of simply walking in a forest with one of Myanmar's most respected meditation teachers.

"Tell me about your meditation practice," he said as they continued deeper into the green cathedral of bamboo and vine.

"I've been practicing for about six years, primarily mindfulness and concentration techniques derived from the Theravada tradition, though I've also explored Zen approaches and some contemporary secular adaptations based on neuroscientific research into—"

"No." His voice cut through her academic recitation with surgical precision. "Not what you've read about meditation. Not the techniques you've studied or the research you've conducted. What actually happens when you sit quietly and attempt to observe your mind?"

The question exposed exactly what she'd hoped to avoid acknowledging during this first meeting. Her actual meditation practice, as opposed to her theoretical knowledge about meditation, was embarrassingly inconsistent and largely ineffective.

"I..." Sarah felt heat creeping up her neck. "I struggle with consistency. My mind wanders constantly. I find myself analyzing the experience instead of having it."

For the first time since meeting him, she saw something that might have been approval in Venerable Thura's eyes. "Honesty. This is the first requirement for any real training."

He stopped walking and turned to face her fully, his attention focusing with laser intensity on something he seemed to see in her expression. "Dr. Chen, I have worked with many Western academics over the years. Most arrive convinced their intellectual understanding is equivalent to wisdom. They want to add meditation to their existing identity rather than allowing meditation to dissolve the identity they think they are."

"I'm not sure I understand the difference."

"The consciousness you research at your university operates on a fundamental assumption, yes? That consciousness is produced by the brain, that awareness emerges from neural activity, that the mind is essentially a biological computer processing information." His words came with the precision of someone who had clearly thought deeply about the philosophical foundations of Western science. "This assumption underlies all of neuroscience, cognitive psychology, artificial intelligence research—your entire academic field."

"That's the prevailing materialist paradigm, though there are emerging theories about consciousness that suggest more complex relationships between mind and brain, quantum theories of consciousness, integrated information theory—"

"Theories." Venerable Thura stopped walking entirely, creating a moment of stillness that seemed to encompass the entire forest around them. "You keep introducing yourself as 'Dr. Chen' as if that title means something here. Tell me, what exactly did that PhD teach you about consciousness? How to measure it? Categorize it? Turn direct experience into publishable data? Your entire field has spent decades studying awareness while remaining completely unconscious. Why should I trust that you're any different?"

The challenge presented intellectual precision that made it impossible to dismiss as Eastern mysticism or a cultural difference. Sarah found herself facing a direct philosophical confrontation with someone who clearly understood her field as well as she did, possibly better.

"That would mean..." She worked through the implications, her mind racing through the cascade of assumptions that would need to be abandoned. "That would require reconsidering the foundation of everything I've studied, everything I've published, my entire professional identity."

"Yes," he said with the simplicity of someone stating an obvious fact. "But before we discuss what you might need to abandon, I need to know what you are actually seeking. Are you hoping to enhance Sarah Chen, the successful professor, by adding some exotic spiritual credentials to your existing achievements? Or are you willing to discover what remains when Sarah Chen—along with all her accomplishments and identities—dissolves completely?"

The question hung in the humid air between them like incense smoke, permeating the space with implications that seemed to reach into the very core of her being. Sarah realized this wasn't just an interview about her meditation background or academic qualifications—it was a fundamental choice about the direction of her entire life.

Her throat felt dry. The sounds of insects and distant temple bells seemed to fade as the weight of his question settled. "I don't know," she admitted, the honesty surprising her with its completeness. "But I think I need to find out."

Venerable Thura nodded slowly, the movement carrying satisfaction that suggested her uncertainty was exactly the response he'd been hoping for. "Good. Not knowing is where all genuine learning begins."

The Quarters

They walked back toward the residential area in comfortable silence, passing monks engaged in various activities that blended work and meditation into a seamless whole. A group tended vegetable gardens with the same attention they might bring to formal sitting practice. Another was repairing the thatched roof of a storage building, each movement deliberate and mindful.

Min Thant waited near a modest wooden building set slightly apart from the main monastery complex, her purple suitcase standing like a neon monument to Western efficiency beside traditional wooden architecture.

"The international residence," Min Thant explained as they approached. "Currently housing six practitioners from various countries—some here for intensive retreat periods of a few months, others for years of systematic training. Venerable Thura accepts students based on readiness rather than calendar availability."

The building reflected the same architectural fusion she'd noticed throughout the compound—British colonial engineering supporting traditional Burmese craftsmanship. Wide verandas provided protection from monsoon rains while allowing air circulation in the tropical climate.

Sarah's room proved spartanly functional: a narrow bed with a thin mattress, a small wooden table, shelves for books and personal items, and little else.

A large window overlooked the garden, wooden shutters propped open to admit the sounds of monastery life. Distant chanting rose and fell like musical prayer. Temple bells marked time according to contemplative rather than commercial rhythms. Conversations in Burmese flowed with melodic cadences of people who had learned to speak without hurry.

The absence of electrical outlets suddenly made her realize how dependent she'd become on constant connectivity to the digital world she'd temporarily left behind.

She set her suitcase on the narrow bed and began unpacking with the systematic approach she brought to most organizational tasks. Laptop first, then chargers, then notebooks filled with research materials, then the digital recorder that had seemed essential for capturing insights that might emerge during contemplative practice.

Min Thant watched without judgment, but his presence made each item feel increasingly irrelevant to whatever was about to unfold in this place. The laptop's sleek design and technological sophistication seemed particularly out of place in a room where the most advanced device was an oil lamp, designed for evening illumination.

When Sarah hesitated over her digital recorder, Min Thant spoke quietly. "Venerable Thura asked me to tell you something. He said the consciousness you seek to study cannot be captured by any device you've brought with you. Your Western academic training has prepared you to examine everything except the one who is doing the examining."

Sarah looked up from her unpacking, meeting his eyes for the first time since arriving. "That sounds like a riddle."

"Perhaps. But he also said that if you can discover who is asking these questions about consciousness, you will understand more than all your research has taught you." Min Thant's expression held a slight smile that suggested vast depths of understanding held lightly. "He tends to begin teaching before students realize lessons have started."

First Evening

That evening, after participating in community meditation—forty minutes of sitting that felt like four hours of wrestling with a mind that refused to settle—Sarah found herself alone with Venerable Thura in the garden behind her quarters.

The air carried the evening sounds of tropical insects and distant chanting from the main hall where some monks continued their practice late into the night. Oil lamps placed strategically throughout the garden created pools of warm light that made electric illumination seem harsh by comparison.

"You seem troubled," Venerable Thura observed, settling onto a wooden bench positioned to overlook the valley below. The simple statement somehow invited confession rather than polite deflection.

Sarah's hands twisted in her lap. "I keep wondering if this is a terrible mistake." The words came faster now, as if released by the day's accumulated tension. "I have tenure, research funding, fifteen years of building a life that makes sense. What if I can't do this kind of training? What if I'm completely wrong about myself?"

For a long moment, Venerable Thura was quiet, his attention

focused on something in the darkening forest that she couldn't see. When he spoke, his voice carried something she hadn't heard before—a quality of personal vulnerability that made her realize she wasn't the only one taking a risk.

"Dr. Chen, in thirty years of teaching, I have guided perhaps two hundred students through various levels of consciousness training. You want to know why I'm pushing you so hard? It's because I've failed with most of the students who have come here. Brilliant people, dedicated people—they either got lost in spiritual fantasies or couldn't handle returning to ordinary life. Three had complete breakdowns. One never spoke coherently again. So when you sit there asking me for reassurance, what you're really asking is whether I can guarantee you won't become another casualty of this work. I can't. No one can.

His fingers traced the edge of the wooden bench as he spoke, the first time she'd seen his hands anything less than perfectly still. "The training I am offering you has never been given to a Western academic. You represent an experiment that could either bridge two worlds or fail completely."

"Why take the risk?"

"Because your world is approaching a crisis point where intellectual understanding of consciousness will not be sufficient. Your species needs people who can demonstrate that awakening is possible within modern life, not just in monasteries removed from contemporary challenges." His eyes met hers with unexpected intensity. "But when this training becomes difficult—and it will become more difficult than anything you have experienced—when every instinct tells you to return to the safety of academic analysis, will you continue? Because if you quit halfway through this process, you will be more lost than when you arrived."

Sarah's mouth went dry. The implications of his words seemed to echo in the humid night air like temple bells. She was being asked to commit not just to a meditation retreat or extended study abroad, but to a fundamental transformation of her understanding of reality itself.

"I'll stay," she said quietly, surprised by the certainty in her voice. "Whatever happens."

Venerable Thura studied her face in the dim light of the oil lamps, his gaze seeming to penetrate layers of identity she'd constructed over thirty-five years of careful self-development. Then, for the first time since her arrival, she saw him smile—not the polite welcome of earlier interactions, but something that looked almost like relief.

"Then we begin tomorrow."

CHAPTER 3: THE UNRAVELING

THE MONASTERY BELL SHATTERED SARAH'S SLEEP AT three-thirty with the metallic insistence of bronze awakening consciousness from dreams where she had been endlessly defending her dissertation before a committee of meditating professors who responded to her academic arguments with profound silence. She jolted upright in the narrow bed, her mind immediately cataloguing the day's agenda with efficiency that had carried her through fifteen years of scholarly productivity: morning sitting, walking meditation, breakfast consumed in silence, individual instruction with Venerable Thura.

But as she swung her feet to the wooden floor, her body protested with aches she didn't recognize as belonging to her usually reliable physical form. Her legs burned from yesterday's failed attempt at lotus position, muscles complaining about arrangements they had never been asked to accept. Her neck had kinked from sleeping on a pillow as thin as guilt, and her stomach cramped with hunger that felt existentially inappropriate for someone pursuing spiritual development rather than mere survival.

Through her window, the monastery compound stirred to life in pre-dawn darkness that felt more alive than any urban morning she had experienced. Robed figures moved between buildings like shadows given purpose and direction, their steps so quiet she could barely distinguish footfalls from the settling sounds of wood responding to temperature changes. Oil lamps flickered in distant windows, creating pools of warm light that made her electric reading lamp seem harsh and invasive—technology that announced its presence rather than serving quietly.

Sarah dressed in loose cotton clothes that had seemed practical in Seattle's climate-controlled environments but now felt like costume pieces in a performance she didn't understand how to give. The mirror above her washbasin reflected someone who looked increasingly displaced from familiar contexts—hair escaping its careful professional arrangement, skin already showing effects of humidity and unfamiliar food, eyes holding the particular exhaustion of someone whose conceptual framework was being systematically dismantled by direct experience.

The meditation hall hummed with concentration when she arrived, forty monks arranged in perfect rows like human tuning forks resonating at frequencies of sustained attention that she could feel even from the doorway. Venerable Thura sat at the hall's front, his stillness so complete he seemed carved from the same teak as the Buddha statue behind him, both forms radiating presence that suggested centuries of patient development.

Sarah attempted to settle into the lotus position that surrounded her, but her Western joints rebelled with the immediacy of a system designed for entirely different arrangements. Her left ankle locked at an angle that sent shooting pains up her calf like electric reminders of her anatomical foreignness. Her right knee refused to descend past a forty-five-degree angle, creating a lopsided arrangement that made sustained stillness feel impossible rather than natural.

This is absurd, her mind announced with authority, bringing to all assessments challenging her competence. *You can't meditate effectively if you can't achieve proper posture. You need appropriate equipment—chairs, cushions, supports designed for Western anatomy. This is precisely the kind of cultural inflexibility that makes Eastern practices inaccessible to serious Western practitioners.*

But there were no chairs in the meditation hall, no benches or cushions designed to accommodate anatomical differences, no concessions to physical limitations that might interfere with contemplative development. There was only the wooden floor, thin mats providing minimal cushioning, and the implicit invitation to work with whatever discomfort arose without immediately seeking escape or accommodation.

Venerable Thura began the morning teaching in Pali, the ancient language rolling off his tongue like water over stones worn smooth by centuries of similar devotional utterances. Sarah understood nothing literal, but something in the cadence touched places in her awareness that academic language had never reached, syllables that seemed designed to bypass rational comprehension and speak directly to whatever listened beneath the mind's constant commentary.

Breath Meditation

She tried to follow her breath, implementing the most basic instruction in every meditation manual she had read with scholarly precision. *In breath, out breath. Simply observe the natural rhythm without attempting to control or modify the process.* But her attention fragmented immediately into multiple streams of simultaneous analysis competing for dominance like television channels broadcasting different programs through the same speaker.

Later, Venerable Thura addressed her difficulties directly: "Your mind creates commentary because you're watching the breath as an object of study rather than merging with the breath as a living process. This is the difference between scientific observation and meditative absorption."

"Try this modification: Instead of watching the breath at your nostrils, breathe as if your entire body is breathing. Feel air entering through your skin, your back, your feet. This prevents the mind from creating an observer-observed duality that generates analysis."

"When thoughts arise—and they will—don't try to stop them or return to the breath. Instead, notice the awareness that recognizes 'thinking is happening.' Rest in THAT awareness. The breath will naturally return to your attention when you stop trying to control the process.

"Signs you're practicing correctly: thoughts slow down naturally without effort, your body feels both relaxed and alert, and time seems to move differently—either very fast or very slow. If you're struggling or feeling tension, you're working too hard. Meditation is more like falling asleep than solving a problem."

The inhalation lasts approximately 3.2 seconds, and the exhalation lasts 4.1 seconds—an interesting variation from standard ratios reported in contemplative literature. The sensation is strongest at the nostrils, though some traditions emphasize abdominal focus. It is essential to note these cultural variables in breathing instruction when documenting this experience for future research applications.

Even as she observed this mental proliferation with growing horror, another part of her mind was cataloguing the observation itself, creating recursive loops of awareness watching awareness watching breathing that generated more mental activity than a graduate seminar on attention regulation psychology. She was studying her meditation rather than meditating, transforming immediate experience into data for future analysis rather than resting in present-moment awareness.

Her left leg went completely numb.

The numbness began as tingling that felt like champagne bubbles under her skin, progressed to burning that suggested nerve damage might be occurring, then descended into an absence of sensation that made her wonder if permanent disability was the price of spiritual development. Her mind immediately generated catastrophic scenarios with the creativity it usually reserved for academic problem-solving: blood clots, circulation shutdown, the irony of acquiring physical limitations while pursuing consciousness expansion.

This is insane, her internal voice announced with increasing volume and authority. *Meditation isn't supposed to be torture disguised as spiritual practice. You're damaging yourself for the sake of cultural authenticity that has nothing to do with genuine contemplative development. Stand up, move around, and use basic common sense about physical limitations.*

But around her, forty monks sat in perfect stillness despite discomfort that must surely exceed her own if they had been maintaining these positions for decades rather than days. Some had been training their bodies to serve contemplative development since childhood, learning to find grace in arrangements that her anatomy experienced as punishment for unknown crimes against proper posture.

Sarah gritted her teeth and endured, her awareness becoming a battlefield between the impulse to escape and the determination to persevere that had carried her through graduate school and academic challenges that had seemed impossible at the time. Sweat beaded on her forehead despite the morning coolness that made the air feel like silk against exposed skin. Her breathing became shallow and rapid, the natural rhythm disrupted by physical stress that transformed meditation into an endurance trial.

The meditation hall began to feel like a crucible designed to separate spiritual commitment from mere intellectual curiosity. On this testing ground, theoretical understanding confronted the reality of sustained practice that demanded more than conceptual appreciation. Every minute felt like an hour spent wrestling with questions about whether contemplative development required accepting discomfort that Western culture had learned to avoid through technological solutions.

When the bell finally released them from sitting with three bronze notes that seemed to dissolve tension throughout the entire compound, Sarah struggled to stand on legs that refused to support her weight with usual reliability. She gripped the wall for balance, pins and needles shooting through her awakening circulation like electric accusations of her physical inadequacy for serious contemplative practice.

Min Thant appeared beside her with the natural helpfulness she was beginning to recognize as monastic training that had transformed compassion from sentiment into practical skill. His assistance felt offered rather than imposed, creating space for her dignity while acknowledging the reality of the transition between different worlds of expectation about how bodies should function.

"Difficult?" he asked, steadying her elbow as sensation returned to her feet with the gradual warmth of circulation resuming its natural patterns.

"Impossible," Sarah gasped, ashamed of her weakness but unable to pretend otherwise in the face of such obvious physical rebellion against contemplative requirements.

"Yes," Min Thant agreed with a smile that contained no mockery, only the recognition of someone who had navigated similar challenges during his own early training. "At first, sitting meditation is like trying to hold water in your hands. The harder you grip, the more quickly it escapes between your fingers."

They walked to the dining hall, Sarah's steps tentative on borrowed legs, as her nervous system adjusted after stillness challenged her sense of comfort.

The morning air carried scents of jasmine and wood smoke, the sounds of monastery life resuming its daily rhythm with the unhurried precision of people who had learned to live according to contemplative rather than commercial schedules. Monks moved between buildings with the same graceful economy she had observed the previous day, their activities seeming to emerge from silence rather than break it with unnecessary urgency.

The Physical Reality of Awakening

The physical challenges of monastery life permeated every aspect of daily existence. Sarah's relationship with her monastery bed had evolved through distinct phases: denial (surely this was temporary), bargaining (maybe if she folded her clothes as padding), anger (who designed furniture as a spiritual practice?), and finally acceptance—though acceptance in this case meant acknowledging that she would spend the next several months feeling like she'd been gently but consistently beaten by enlightened bamboo.

Her Western body, accustomed to memory foam and ergonomic design, filed nightly complaints that her academic mind dutifully catalogued: lower back pains, hip joint grievances, shoulder blade objections. She'd spent years studying the relationship between physical comfort and consciousness, but apparently, understanding and embodying were completely different skill sets.

"The bed is teaching you something," Venerable Thura mentioned during one of their morning conversations as Sarah rubbed her lower back with obvious discomfort.

"Yes," she replied, "that I'm materialistic, soft, and possibly too old for this."

"That too," he agreed with uncharacteristic directness. "But also impermanence. Every moment of discomfort will pass. Every moment of comfort will also pass. The question is: what remains constant?"

Sarah considered this wisdom while secretly planning to ship herself a mattress topper. Despite his teachings about impermanence, her restless mind still drifted to worldly concerns—work emails accumulating in her absence like digital snow that would require hours of clearing, conference papers that needed finishing, academic responsibilities that seemed increasingly surreal in this context where time moved according to entirely different principles than productivity and efficiency.

Breakfast as Practice

In the dining hall, breakfast was served in wooden bowls that felt substantial in ways her usual ceramic dishware had never achieved—rice porridge with dried fish, vegetables she couldn't identify, prepared with techniques that transformed simple ingredients into flavors that spoke of patience and attention applied to basic nutrition. The monks ate in silence, each spoonful consumed with the same mindful concentration they brought to meditation, as though feeding the body were another form of contemplative practice rather than mere biological necessity.

No one rushed through their meal, and no one seemed preoccupied with finishing quickly to move on to more important activities. The absence of conversation created space for attention to focus on immediate experience—the texture of rice against her tongue, the complex mineral taste of well water, the subtle satisfaction that came from eating without distraction or hurry.

Sarah tried to match their pace, but her Western conditioning insisted that eating was a utilitarian function rather than a contemplative opportunity. The rice porridge was bland by her usual standards, unseasoned and unfamiliar to a palate accustomed to complex restaurant flavors and processed foods that announced themselves with artificial intensity. But as she continued eating in silence, guided by the example of practitioners who had learned to find satisfaction in simplicity, subtle tastes began to emerge like hidden music becoming audible to more refined listening.

Rice's natural sweetness revealed itself gradually, along with the mineral complexity of water drawn from wells that had served the monastery for generations. Textures that had seemed monotonous began to reveal variety that could only be appreciated through unhurried attention—the way each grain maintained its individual character while contributing to collective nourishment, the satisfaction that came from food consumed mindfully rather than mechanically.

Practical Humility

After breakfast, Sarah discovered that monastery life extended its lessons into every practical necessity. She approached the well with the confidence of someone who had mastered complex laboratory equipment, only to find herself engaged in an unexpectedly humbling physics experiment.

Sarah stared at the well bucket and rope, her academic mind cycling through water retrieval physics while her bladder offered increasingly urgent commentary. After three attempts that left her soaked and no closer to basic hygiene, she understood why the monks moved with such deliberate precision—it wasn't spiritual mindfulness, it was survival.

"Dr. Chen," Min Thant appeared beside her with perfect timing, "perhaps I could demonstrate the proper technique?"

Sarah nodded with the dignity of someone who had published papers on consciousness while being defeated by a bucket.

With basic hygiene finally achieved through Min Thant's patient instruction, the morning's formal practice continues.

In the meditation hall, Venerable Thura gestured toward a cushion arranged before the simple altar where incense smoke traced lazy spirals toward the wooden ceiling.

"Simply observe the breath," Venerable Thura instructed with the casual tone of someone suggesting she check the weather.

Sarah's mind immediately launched into analysis mode: respiratory rate, diaphragmatic movement, oxygen saturation levels. She was documenting her breathing so thoroughly that she forgot to actually breathe, resulting in a meditation session that resembled marine biology research more than spiritual practice.

When she opened her eyes, gasping slightly, Venerable Thura was regarding her with patient amusement.

"Perhaps less observation, more breathing?" he suggested.

Walking Meditation

After the sitting practice, walking meditation awaited.

Venerable Thura led them to a covered walkway that bordered the compound's main garden, where morning light filtered through leaves that created patterns of illumination and shadow across the stone path worn smooth by decades of contemplative steps. "Thirty steps forward," he instructed in English, apparently for Sarah's benefit rather than the monks who had practiced this routine for years. "Turn with complete attention. Thirty steps back. Very slowly, with awareness given entirely to each movement."

Sarah watched the monks begin their practice, their steps so deliberate they seemed to be conducting conversations with the earth itself through the soles of their bare feet. Each foot lifted, moved forward, and descended with ceremonial precision, as though walking were a form of prayer that required perfect articulation of intention through physical movement.

She joined the line of practitioners, attempting to match their pace while her mind immediately began planning the endpoint of each journey, calculating how long the walking period would last, and anticipating the moment when they would return to sitting practice. Her feet moved automatically while her attention scattered in every direction except the immediate experience of placing one foot in front of the other with conscious intention.

This is pointless, her analytical mind complained with the authority it brought to all activities that challenged its dominance. *Walking is the most basic human activity. You've been walking just fine for thirty-five years without needing special instruction. This artificial slowness is spiritual theater designed to make simple activities seem profound through exotic presentation.*

But even as these thoughts arose with their familiar critical commentary, Sarah noticed something else happening beneath the surface criticism that usually dominated her response to unfamiliar practices. The extreme slowness was revealing layers of experience usually obscured by habitual momentum—the complex balance adjustments that usually occurred below conscious awareness, the way each step required dozens of muscle coordinations she had never appreciated, the moment-by-moment choices about direction and pace that shaped movement through space.

"Slower," Venerable Thura whispered as he passed her in the line, his voice seeming to arise from the silence itself rather than breaking it with instruction. "Each step should require ten seconds. When you think you are moving slowly enough, reduce that speed by half."

Ten seconds per step felt absurd, like meditation designed by people who had never experienced the practical requirements of efficient transportation. But Sarah attempted to comply with the instruction, immediately discovering that her usual walking pace had been a form of unconsciousness—movement designed to transport her from one place to another without any attention to the process itself.

At normal speed, walking was simply transportation from point A to point B, a mechanical function that served other purposes rather than deserving attention in its own right. At contemplative speed, walking became a microscopic exploration of movement itself, each shift of weight and adjustment of balance revealing complexity that had been invisible when covered by efficiency and speed.

Her mind rebelled against the artificial constraint with increasing creativity, generating elaborate justifications for resuming normal pace that drew on her academic understanding of time management and productive use of limited retreat opportunities. *Your time is limited here. You could be learning advanced meditation techniques instead of wasting hours on glorified walking exercises. This is precisely the kind of exotic nonsense that gives contemplative practice a bad reputation in serious academic circles.*

But beneath the mental resistance, something else was stirring like recognition awakening after a long sleep. The extreme slowness was creating space between intention and action, between thought and response, between the impulse to move and movement itself. In that space, awareness could observe the usually invisible processes by which the mind created experience and translated intention into physical manifestation.

After an hour of walking meditation that covered perhaps fifty yards of total distance, Sarah's legs trembled with fatigue despite the minimal physical demands of such abbreviated movement. The monks had made the practice look effortless, but she discovered that conscious movement required far more energy than unconscious transportation, attention-demanding resources that automatic functioning had never needed.

"Now sitting practice," Venerable Thura announced, leading them back to the meditation hall where cushions waited with the patience of objects that had supported decades of contemplative development.

Sarah's heart sank like a stone dropped into deep water. Her body had barely recovered from the morning's ordeal of enforced stillness, and the prospect of returning to that lotus-position torture chamber felt like deliberate cruelty designed to test her commitment through unnecessary suffering. But there seemed to be no alternative except admitting defeat on her second day of what was supposed to be a week-long investigation into consciousness.

This time, Venerable Thura positioned himself directly across from her, his presence both reassuring and intimidating—like being personally observed by consciousness itself during its investigation of its own nature. He gestured for her to close her eyes and begin following her breath with the same careful attention she had attempted during the morning session.

But now, primed by the walking meditation's lessons about the space between intention and action, Sarah noticed something she had missed before in all her previous attempts at breath-following meditation. The breath she was trying to follow was already breathing itself without requiring conscious management or control. Her lungs expanded and contracted according to rhythms more ancient than thought. Her heart beat without needing instruction from the mind that insisted on controlling everything.

Blood circulated through vessels that knew their pathways without consulting maps. Cells metabolized nutrients according to processes that had been refined over millions of years of evolution. Her nervous system processed thousands of inputs every second without requiring conscious supervision or management. The body maintained itself through intelligence that vastly exceeded anything her rational mind could comprehend or control.

"Who is breathing?" Venerable Thura asked softly, his voice seeming to arise from the space between inhalation and exhalation rather than from any particular location in the meditation hall.

The question stopped Sarah's mental commentary with the precision of a circuit breaker protecting electrical systems from overload. She had been trying to observe her breath, but who exactly was the observer conducting this observation? The thought that attempted to follow breathing was itself arising and passing away like clouds in an empty sky, temporary formations in awareness that had no solid substance of its own.

The awareness that noticed thoughts seemed to have no thoughts of their own, no agenda or investment in any particular experience or outcome. It was like discovering a room in her house she had never noticed—familiar yet unknown, ordinary yet extraordinary, always present but somehow overlooked despite decades of occupying the same consciousness.

For perhaps thirty seconds, Sarah's attention rested in this space between observer and observed, between the one who meditated and meditation itself. It felt like finding the eye of a hurricane—perfect stillness at the center of activity that continued spinning without disturbing the peace at its core. The experience carried qualities of recognition rather than achievement, as though she were remembering something always present rather than developing something new.

Then her mind reasserted its familiar patterns with the efficiency of systems returning to default settings after temporary disruption. *Interesting phenomenological observation. Possible dissolution of subject-object duality, though could also be explained as simple attention stabilization. Need to examine this more carefully, perhaps correlate with EEG data from similar states documented in contemplative literature.*

The analytical commentary collapsed whatever space had opened, returning her to the familiar struggle between the one trying to meditate and meditation that seemed perpetually just out of reach. The peace she had glimpsed disappeared like water absorbed by sand, leaving only the memory of something significant that had occurred too briefly to understand or sustain.

When the session ended with bells that seemed to emerge from silence itself rather than being produced by metal struck by human hands, Venerable Thura remained seated while the other monks dispersed to their various daily activities. Sarah found it difficult to stand, as her legs were not just numb, but completely uncooperative. She needed to use the wall for support to finally get upright, which felt like a victory over her own body.

"Better," Venerable Thura observed without apparent irony, his assessment carrying weight that made her question whether she understood what constituted progress in contemplative development.

"Better?" Sarah looked at him with disbelief that bordered on indignation. "I spent the entire session fighting with my mind like amateur wrestling with professional opponents. I couldn't sustain attention for more than a few seconds without distraction. I was analyzing instead of experiencing, thinking instead of being present with immediate awareness."

"Yes," he agreed with obvious satisfaction, as though her struggles represented significant advancement rather than evidence of fundamental incompetence. "And you noticed this pattern. Yesterday, you were simply analyzing without awareness of the analyzing process itself. Today, awareness began to recognize its own activity. This represents genuine progress."

"But I'm not getting anywhere," Sarah complained with the annoyance of someone who's used to seeing evident progress toward specific goals. "I'm not developing the concentration your tradition describes as fundamental to contemplative development. I'm not experiencing the calm states that your students seem to achieve through sustained practice."

Venerable Thura's smile contained the patience of someone who had guided countless meditators through identical frustrations, each seeker discovering the same obstacles and opportunities that characterized human consciousness investigating itself.

"You are trying to meditate from the wrong location," he said with the gentleness of someone correcting a simple but fundamental error. "Like someone standing in a river complaining that they cannot find water anywhere in their environment."

"I don't understand what you mean."

"The awareness that notices distraction is not distracted," he explained with the precision of someone pointing out something obvious that had somehow been overlooked. "The consciousness that observes thinking is not caught in thoughts themselves. You have been trying to achieve a state of meditation instead of recognizing the awareness that is already present, already peaceful, already free from the problems your mind creates through its efforts to solve them."

Sarah stared at him, feeling both illuminated and confused by instructions that seemed to point toward something simple yet completely elusive. "But surely there are deeper states to develop? Higher levels of consciousness to achieve through sustained practice and proper technique?"

"Perhaps," Venerable Thura said, rising with his characteristic effortlessness that suggested movement without effort or intention. "But first, learn to recognize the consciousness you already are rather than trying to become something you imagine you are not. Otherwise, you will spend years attempting to develop what was never absent, trying to achieve what you have never stopped being."

That afternoon, alone in her simple quarters while heat pressed against the windows like something alive seeking entrance, Sarah sat with her journal for the first time since arriving. She had planned to document her retreat experiences with scholarly precision, creating detailed observations that could inform future research and possibly contribute to papers on the phenomenology of contemplative development.

But now, staring at the blank page with pen motionless in her hand, she found herself without words for what was occurring. How did one describe the space between thoughts using thought itself? How could academic language capture the quality of awareness that notices awareness without becoming another object of analysis? Her usual vocabulary of neural correlates, altered states, and consciousness development felt increasingly inadequate for experiences that seemed to exist outside the categories structuring her professional understanding.

She began writing: "Day Two: Traditional meditation instruction proves more challenging than research suggested. Physical discomfort presents significant barriers to sustained practice. Mental activity continues despite concentrated efforts at attention regulation. Notable phenomenological observation during afternoon sitting session—"

Sarah stopped writing and set the journal aside with the gesture of someone recognizing futility when it appeared. Even here, even now, she was transforming immediate experience into data for future analysis rather than allowing whatever was trying to emerge in the present moment to unfold without interference from her documenting mind.

Outside her window, monastery life continued its unhurried rhythm like music played at the proper tempo rather than rushed for efficiency. Monks moved between buildings with the presence of embodied prayers, their existence seeming to emerge from silence rather than disturb it with unnecessary activity or urgency.

Evening light slanted through bodhi trees, creating patterns of illumination that shifted with each breath of wind like visual demonstrations of impermanence embraced rather than resisted. Temple bells marked time according to contemplative rather than commercial schedules, their bronze voices creating harmony rather than demanding attention.

For the first time since arriving, Sarah allowed herself to simply sit without agenda, without trying to meditate or understand or document anything that might be happening in her awareness. She watched light change across the garden like natural cinema requiring no interpretation or analysis. She listened to distant temple bells with the same receptivity she might bring to music, allowing sound to wash through her consciousness without needing to categorize or explain its effects.

In that simple sitting without purpose or technique, something shifted with the subtlety of a tide changing direction. Not an achievement or attainment that could be grasped or sustained through effort, but a recognition of what had always been present beneath the mind's constant activity. The awareness that was experiencing these shifting phenomena was itself peaceful, untroubled by the difficulties her thinking mind created through its efforts to control and understand everything.

It was like discovering that she had been swimming in an ocean while complaining about being thirsty—the very consciousness that struggled with meditation was already the peace she sought through meditation practice. The recognition lasted only moments before her mind resumed its familiar patterns of analysis and planning, but something had been glimpsed that couldn't be unglimpsed.

Beneath all her academic expertise, beneath her meditation struggles, beneath her spiritual ambitions and intellectual understanding, some fundamental okayness remained constant—present whether she noticed it or not, undisturbed by her efforts to develop or achieve or understand anything at all.

That evening, as monastery bells called the community to final prayers and the compound settled into deeper silence that characterized night in places devoted to contemplative development, Sarah lay in her narrow bed listening to sounds of practitioners ending their day with the same unhurried attention they brought to all activities.

Tomorrow promises more walking meditation, challenging every assumption about moving efficiently. Sitting practice will expose the mind's resistance to stillness, and meals eaten in mindful silence will transform nourishment into a contemplative experience. Yet, tonight, she carries a different question into sleep, one that feels more significant than any research hypothesis she has ever devised.

What if awakening wasn't about becoming someone who could meditate successfully, but about recognizing the awareness that had never needed to meditate because it was already the peace that meditation promised to deliver? What if consciousness development meant not developing consciousness at all, but simply discovering the consciousness that had been present throughout every moment of seeking and struggle and apparent progress?

The questions followed her into dreams where she walked endlessly through libraries containing every book about water ever written, searching with increasing desperation for someone who could explain what wetness felt like to someone who had never been dry.

Village Context and Community Integration

The next morning brought her first glimpse of the monastery's intimate relationship with the surrounding community through the daily alms round—a procession down the mountain path toward the village at its base, carrying simple wooden bowls that villagers would fill as part of their daily spiritual practice and economic contribution to contemplative life.

The walk down the mountain took thirty minutes, following a well-worn path that wound between terraced gardens where vegetables grew in careful rows that demonstrated generations of accumulated wisdom about mountain agriculture. Sarah could see why the location had been chosen centuries ago—high enough to provide solitude for intensive practice, but close enough to population centers to maintain the symbiotic relationship that sustained monastic communities throughout Southeast Asia.

Her Western shoes felt clumsy on the uneven stones, each step requiring more attention than she usually devoted to walking. The monks moved with unconscious grace, their bare feet finding stable placement automatically while her sneakers searched for secure footing. Even this simple downhill walk turned into a way to reflect on how to adapt. She had to let go of her usual speed and instead move in a way that respected the land, rather than trying to rush through it.

The village of Pyin Oo Lwin spread across a small valley like a living mandala—houses arranged in rough circles around a central market area. The village monastery served as both a spiritual and a social hub, connecting individual families to larger networks of meaning and mutual support.

Children ran alongside the procession of monks, not begging or demanding attention, but simply sharing in the joy of a daily ritual that connected their community with the sacred mountain above.

Sarah watched villagers emerge from their homes carrying rice, curry, fruit, and simple sweets—enough to feed forty monks and their lay practitioners for the day, provided freely as part of a spiritual practice that understood material giving as an expression of non-attachment and recognition of interconnection. But the exchange felt like much more than an economic transaction or a religious obligation.

Each offering was made with hands pressed together in respectful greeting, often accompanied by brief blessings spoken in soft Burmese that carried genuine affection and gratitude for the monastery's presence in their community. The monks received each gift with equal dignity, whether it came from the wealthy shop owner who could afford elaborate curry preparations or the elderly woman who offered only a handful of rice and a single banana with apologies for her family's current economic difficulties.

"The villagers receive merit from offering food," Min Thant explained as they followed the procession through narrow streets where traditional wooden houses displayed the intricate carving that demonstrated centuries of accumulated artistic wisdom. "But the monks receive something equally valuable—connection with the community they serve, and a reminder that spiritual practice must benefit worldly life, not escape from everyday responsibilities and relationships."

Meeting the Community

At the village market, Sarah was introduced to several key

families who had supported the monastery for generations, their children growing up with a natural understanding that contemplative practice and community service were inseparable aspects of meaningful life.

Daw Soe, an elderly woman who ran a small grocery stall, spoke enough English to share stories about miraculous healings that had occurred when monastery practitioners worked with village children whose problems exceeded local medical resources.

"My grandson, very sick two years ago," she explained while arranging fruit displays with the artistic attention that transformed ordinary commerce into aesthetic practice. "Doctors in Yangon say nothing can help, maybe brain problem from birth. Family bring him to mountain monastery, foreign student there teach him special meditation. Now he completely normal, even better than normal—very intelligent, very kind to other children."

Sarah felt her academic skepticism engage automatically, searching for rational explanations for what sounded like impossible claims. But something in Daw Soe's matter-of-fact delivery, combined with the apparent health and intelligence of the boy playing nearby, made her usual analytical responses feel less relevant than simple listening.

U Tin, the village medical officer, described how monastery training had influenced his approach to healthcare, teaching him to address emotional and spiritual aspects of illness alongside physical symptoms that conventional medicine could treat with available resources. His small clinic had become an integration point where traditional healing wisdom combined with contemporary medical knowledge to serve patient needs that neither approach could address independently.

"Western medicine very good for emergency treatment, broken bones, infectious disease," he explained during their conversation in his clinic that contained both modern medical equipment and traditional healing implements. "But many illnesses have psychological roots, spiritual causes that medicine cannot touch. When monastery practitioners work with patients, healing happens at levels that medical science does not understand but cannot deny."

The conversation challenged Sarah's materialist perspective in ways that felt both uncomfortable and intriguing. As a consciousness researcher, she was familiar with psychosomatic healing and the mind-body connection, but U Tin spoke of interventions that seemed to transcend conventional understanding of those relationships.

Extended Family Networks

It was her meeting with Min Thant's extended family that revealed the depth of monastery-village integration and the practical ways that contemplative training served community development beyond individual spiritual advancement.

His aunt, Ma Thandar, managed a small lending cooperative that provided micro-finance to village women starting small businesses—selling vegetables, weaving textiles, raising chickens for eggs and meat. But the lending circles operated according to principles learned through Buddhist practice, emphasizing mutual support and shared prosperity rather than individual profit maximization.

"We learned from monastery teachings that true wealth comes from everyone's success, not just personal accumulation," Ma Thandar explained as they sat in her modest home, decorated with flowers from her garden and family photos that showed three generations of monastery supporters. "When one family prospers, whole community becomes stronger. When community is strong, each family has more security and opportunity."

Min Thant's uncle, U Aung, had adapted meditation techniques to improve agricultural productivity, teaching farmers how contemplative awareness could help them read soil conditions, weather patterns, and plant health with sensitivity that supplemented technical agricultural knowledge. His innovations had increased crop yields while reducing dependence on expensive fertilizers and pesticides that many families couldn't afford.

"Meditation teaches you to pay attention," U Kyaw said

simply. "When you really see plants, soil, sky, you understand what they need. Modern agriculture looks only at chemicals and machinery, but traditional wisdom includes consciousness as farming tool."

Sarah began to understand that the monastery wasn't separate from worldly concerns but deeply engaged with them through approaches that honored both spiritual principles and practical necessities. The contemplative training she was about to begin existed within this larger context of service, not as an escape from worldly responsibilities.

Understanding Mutual Service

As they climbed back up the mountain path, Sarah reflected on what she had witnessed. The relationship between monastery and village challenged her assumptions about religious life as withdrawal from society. Instead, she had observed integration that seemed to benefit both communities through exchanges that transcended simple economic transactions.

"You look puzzled," Min Thant observed as they paused to rest beside a shrine where incense smoke carried prayers into the afternoon air.

"I expected the monastery to be more... separate," Sarah admitted. "In the West, spiritual retreats usually mean isolation from daily concerns. But you seem deeply involved with village life, even dependent on it."

"Individual enlightenment without compassionate service is just sophisticated selfishness," Min Thant replied with the directness that seemed characteristic of monastery communication. "We practice here not to escape the world's suffering but to develop capacities that can relieve it. The village's well-being and our spiritual development are inseparable."

He gestured toward the valley below, where afternoon light revealed the intricate networks of relationships that connected every household to larger patterns of mutual support. "Your training will develop extraordinary abilities—meditation techniques that can produce remarkable results. But all of it serves this larger purpose of reducing suffering and increasing wisdom, not just for yourself but for everyone whose life you touch."

As they reached the monastery gates, Sarah realized that her academic research into consciousness had never prepared her for this understanding of spiritual development as community service. She had come seeking personal transformation, but she was beginning to glimpse training that aimed toward something much larger than individual attainment.

Her journey was just beginning, but already the scope felt both more demanding and more inspiring than anything she had imagined possible.

CHAPTER 4: THE LIGHT BEARER

First Level Training: Light Generation (Tejomaya)

The breakthrough had changed everything and nothing.

Sarah sat in the forest meditation hut where she had first glimpsed her own luminosity three days earlier, staring at her hands as though they belonged to someone else. The memory felt simultaneously vivid and impossible—warmth spreading through her chest during loving-kindness meditation for her parents, then the soft golden glow that had illuminated the bamboo walls for exactly ten minutes before her excitement had scattered it like smoke.

Since then, nothing. Her palms remained stubbornly ordinary, despite hours of attempted replication; her academic mind catalogued each failed attempt with the methodical precision that had once made her successful in research, but now felt like an obstacle to everything mysterious and transformative.

"The first glimpse is not the accomplishment," Venerable Thura had said when she'd reported her experience. "It is consciousness recognizing its own creative potential. Now we begin the actual cultivation."

And so, despite having experienced the impossible, Sarah

found herself starting over—not as a meditation novice this time, but as a student of something she had no name for, something that existed at the intersection of love, awareness, and what appeared to be direct influence over physical reality.

Week One: Foundations of Luminous Awareness

"Forget everything you think you know about light," Venerable Thura said as they settled into their first formal training session. The morning air carried the scent of jasmine and wood smoke, monastery life awakening around them in familiar rhythms that had become as natural as breathing. "Your Western science understands photons as particles and waves, but traditional training works with light as the creative expression of consciousness itself."

Sarah noticed her analytical mind kicking in even though she aimed to stay open and receptive. After fifteen years of studying consciousness academically from a distance, shifting from observer to practitioner required her to remain alert to old habits of conceptual thinking that hindered direct experience.

"Light generation becomes possible when the meditator recognizes that awareness and energy are the same phenomenon," he continued, settling into the teaching posture she had learned indicated serious transmission. "What you call 'effort' actually creates the appearance of separation between the one who tries and the light that wants to manifest naturally."

The instruction that followed challenged Sarah's understanding of how spiritual abilities were cultivated. Instead of directing energy, visualizing particular forms, or concentrating on specific body centers—techniques she had read about in various meditation manuals during her academic research—she was guided to rest in recognition of awareness while maintaining gentle intention for luminosity to manifest naturally.

"Your scientific training is both helpful and limiting," Venerable Thura observed during a particularly frustrating session where Sarah's attempts to "produce light" had resulted in nothing but physical tension and mental strain. "Helpful because you understand energy and matter are convertible according to principles consciousness can access. Limiting because you approach this as a problem to be solved rather than a nature to be revealed."

The first week became an extended lesson in what Venerable Thura called "effortless effort"—learning to maintain clear intention without forcing results, allowing rather than creating, recognizing rather than producing. Sarah would sit in a meditation posture, acknowledging the space of awareness in which all experiences appeared, and then rest in that recognition while holding a gentle intention for luminosity to manifest, if and when it was natural.

When she noticed herself straining or trying to force particular outcomes, she would relax back into simple presence. When analytical thinking arose to comment on the process or judge her progress, she would return to the foundational recognition that awareness itself was naturally luminous, regardless of whether that luminosity expressed itself in visibly obvious ways.

Day after day, nothing visible occurred. But something subtler was developing—a growing sense that the boundary between her consciousness and the surrounding environment was more permeable than she had ever imagined. During meditation, she began experiencing moments when her awareness seemed to extend beyond the usual bodily boundaries, sensing the life-force energy of trees, plants, and even stones in the forest surrounding the meditation hut.

"The light you seek to generate externally is already shining as your awareness itself," Venerable Thura said during a session where Sarah expressed frustration with her lack of visible progress. "But your attention has been focused on objects within awareness for so long that you have forgotten to recognize the luminosity of awareness itself."

This teaching led to a significant shift in Sarah's understanding of what they were actually practicing. Rather than developing a new ability she didn't currently possess, she was learning to recognize a capacity that had always been present but obscured by habitual patterns of attention that focused on the content of experience rather than the experiencing awareness.

"Western students often approach spiritual practice like learning musical instruments," Venerable Thura continued with the patience she had observed in all his interactions with struggling practitioners. "They expect gradual improvement through repetition and effort, measurable progress that can be tracked and evaluated. But awakening capacities are more like learning to see —once you know how to look, the seeing is immediate and natural."

During the first week, Sarah also began experiencing unusual energy sensations during meditation—tingling in her hands and arms, warmth radiating from her chest, and what felt like subtle electrical currents moving through her nervous system in patterns that seemed to correspond with breath and attention. When she described these phenomena, Venerable Thura's response carried the precision she had learned to associate with his most important teachings.

"These sensations indicate your nervous system is adjusting to support abilities that conventional conditioning has taught you are impossible," he explained. "The physical body must prepare itself to channel consciousness in ways that transcend ordinary limitations. What you are experiencing is natural preparation for capacities that require integration at cellular levels."

By the end of the first week, Sarah could maintain stable recognition of awareness for periods extending beyond thirty minutes without distraction by mental commentary or analytical thinking. Not as an object of attention, but as the subject that was attending—the luminous space in which all objects appeared and disappeared without disturbing the fundamental clarity that witnessed their arising and passing.

However, she had still not generated visible light, and the gap between recognition of awareness and demonstration of abilities was creating doubts about whether the training was actually working or whether she was learning to maintain pleasant meditative states unrelated to the supernatural capacities Venerable Thura had described.

Week Two: Energy and Effort

"Why can some people produce visible luminosity while others cannot?" Sarah asked during their eighth session, voicing concerns that had been building as she heard some monks discussing more dramatic developments in their practice. "Is it a matter of natural talent, or years of preparation I lack?"

"Neither of those," he head twitched in dissent. "Light generation becomes possible when you recognize that awareness and energy are unified. What you call 'effort' creates apparent separation between consciousness and the luminosity that is consciousness expressing its creative nature."

This teaching introduced Sarah to an entirely different approach than anything she had encountered in Western spiritual contexts. Instead of trying harder, concentrating more intensely, or following more complex techniques, she was being asked to relax more completely into recognition that consciousness and luminosity were not different phenomena requiring connection through effort.

The practice sessions became exercises in progressively subtler forms of non-doing. Sarah would rest in a meditation posture, recognize awareness, and maintain a gentle intention for luminosity to manifest, while releasing any sense of being someone who was trying to accomplish something. When she noticed tension or forcing, she would return to simple presence. When thoughts arose to comment on the process, she would acknowledge them and return to the foundational recognition that awareness was naturally creative.

"In Tibetan training, they speak of 'letting luminosity express itself,'" Venerable Thura explained during a teaching session that felt more like poetry than technical instruction. "This refers to consciousness recognizing that creativity is its essential nature. Light generation is not something you do—it is something you allow by stepping out of the way of your own luminous essence."

But the "stepping out of the way" proved more difficult than Sarah had anticipated. Her whole identity was built on achieving through intelligence and systematic effort. The idea that her deepest spiritual capacity could develop by not trying challenged core beliefs about competence, success, and personal control.

During the second week, her practice was constantly disrupted by intrusive thoughts about family back home. In the middle of sessions that should have been focused on luminosity cultivation, her mind would suddenly flood with worries: Had her father's heart condition worsened? How was her mother managing household finances? How was her brother getting on with his job?

The monastery's communication policy—brief weekly text messages to family—amplified her anxiety. Her mother's messages were typically optimistic but vague: "All well here. Dad's follow-up went fine. Hope your studies are progressing. Love."

Each message raised more questions than it answered, and Sarah found herself constructing elaborate scenarios about potential problems that might be developing in her absence. During what should have been pure concentration on luminosity, half her attention was absorbed wondering how her sister was coping with her newborn.

"Family love is not an obstacle to light generation," Venerable Thura observed when Sarah described how thoughts of home were interfering with her practice. "Family love IS luminosity, temporarily appearing as concern for particular individuals. The solution is not to eliminate caring, but to recognize caring as the very luminous energy you are learning to generate."

This reframing transformed Sarah's entire approach. Instead of viewing thoughts about family as distractions from spiritual practice, she began treating them as opportunities to recognize the luminous quality of love itself. When worry about her father arose during meditation, she would feel the love underlying the concern and allow that caring energy to fill her awareness. When anxiety about her sister appeared, she would sense the warmth of affection and let it expand throughout her entire body.

"The breakthrough will come through love, not despite it," Venerable Thura said during a session where Sarah had begun experiencing sustained warmth in her chest while thinking of her parents' well-being. "Western students often believe spiritual development requires abandoning personal attachments. Traditional training recognizes that purified attachment becomes universal compassion, and universal compassion is the source of all genuine spiritual abilities."

By the end of the second week, Sarah was experiencing consistent warmth and energy sensations during meditation, particularly when focusing on loving-kindness for family members. The sensations felt distinctly different from ordinary emotional warmth—more electrical, more expansive, more connected to the fundamental life-force that seemed to animate everything around her.

"These energy experiences indicate your nervous system is preparing to support visible manifestations," Venerable Thura advised, when Sarah described the phenomenon. "But do not try to force the transition from internal sensation to external light. Allow the process to unfold naturally, at its own pace, according to its own wisdom."

Week Three: The Sustained Breakthrough

The sustained breakthrough came during the third week, on a morning when Sarah had abandoned entirely trying to generate light and was enjoying the profound love that had become her natural state during family-focused meditation. She had been sitting for perhaps forty-five minutes, extending loving-kindness toward her parents with the same intensity she had once brought to academic research, when she became aware of subtle changes in the quality of illumination around her.

At first, she assumed it was the oil lamp flickering or perhaps the first hints of dawn beginning to penetrate the bamboo grove. But when she opened her eyes slightly to check, she could see that the familiar flame burned steadily and the sky remained intensely dark beyond the meditation hut's windows. Yet there was definitely more light in the space than the single lamp could account for.

The additional illumination seemed to emanate from the space around her body—not bright enough to read by, but clearly perceptible as soft, golden radiance extending perhaps two feet from her skin in all directions. Sarah felt her heart rate accelerate with excitement, then immediately noticed how the emotional reaction caused the luminosity to fade back to barely perceptible levels.

"Remain in recognition," Venerable Thura said quietly, his voice carrying the same calm precision he maintained regardless of whatever extraordinary phenomena might be manifesting around his students. "Strong emotions create energetic disturbance that interferes with subtle manifestations. Return to simple awareness of awareness itself."

Sarah closed her eyes and returned to the foundational recognition that had become familiar over previous weeks—not focusing on anything particular, but simply resting as the space of consciousness in which all experience appeared. Within minutes, she could sense the gentle radiance beginning to stabilize, no longer dependent on her excitement or anxiety about its presence.

"Now maintain this state for one hour," Venerable Thura instructed. "Do not try to increase the intensity or change anything about what is occurring. Rest in the recognition that allows luminosity to express itself naturally."

The hour that followed was unlike anything Sarah had experienced. The gentle golden light remained stable throughout the session, requiring no effort to maintain once she learned to rest in the awareness that was its source. She could feel the luminosity as clearly as she could feel her heartbeat—not as something she was producing, but as something she was allowing, like stepping out of the way of a river that had constantly been flowing.

When the session concluded, Sarah opened her eyes to find

Venerable Thura regarding her with obvious satisfaction. However, his expression carried none of the surprise she had expected to see in response to such an extraordinary development.

"This is good progress," he said. "Tomorrow we work with sustained generation over longer periods."

Over the following days, Sarah learned to maintain the gentle luminosity for periods extending beyond two hours. The light could be sustained during walking meditation, during meals, even during sleep, becoming less a special state requiring particular conditions than a natural expression of awareness that had learned to recognize its own creative potential.

"The luminosity you can now maintain externally has always been shining as your awareness itself," Venerable Thura explained during a teaching session where Sarah's entire body was glowing with soft golden light. "Individual consciousness and universal luminosity are not different phenomena. What you are discovering is that you are not separate from the creative source of everything you perceive."

But the most significant development was not the visible light itself, but the transformation in Sarah's understanding of identity that accompanied sustained luminosity. When generating light, she did not feel like "Sarah Chen, academic," who had acquired supernatural abilities. She felt like luminous awareness itself, temporarily manifesting through the form of an individual practitioner, but had never actually been separate from universal consciousness.

"Each training level dissolves particular categories of limitation," Venerable Thura said when Sarah described this identity shift. "Light generation specifically addresses the belief that consciousness and energy are separate phenomena. Students who master this training discover that awareness itself is fundamentally creative and luminous."

Week Four: Integration and Testing

The fourth week brought Sarah's first applications of light generation beyond meditation sessions, as Venerable Thura tested her ability to maintain luminous awareness during challenging circumstances that required sustained attention and practical problem-solving.

"Consciousness that can illuminate itself in stillness must learn to illuminate practical activity," he explained as they prepared for what he called "integration training." "Spiritual abilities that function only during formal meditation are interesting but ultimately useless. Real development serves all aspects of life."

The first test came during the hottest day Sarah had experienced in Myanmar. By dawn, the temperature had already climbed beyond thirty-eight degrees Celsius, and the humidity made even minimal physical activity feel like working in a steam bath. Venerable Thura led her to the cave system deep in the mountain, where she had first glimpsed light —a network of tunnels extending far underground.

At the entrance, he handed her an oil lamp, its metal handle already uncomfortable from heat exposure. "Navigate to the deepest chamber and return," he instructed. "But you may not use external light—only the luminosity of consciousness itself."

Sarah stared into the cave's absolute darkness, fear pressing against her ribs like a physical weight. She had produced only gentle glows in meditation, hardly enough to navigate by. Inside the cave's oppressive heat, maintaining concentration would be even more difficult.

"The light you've cultivated in stillness must now serve movement," Venerable Thura said. "Consciousness that can illuminate itself can illuminate anything."

Sarah extinguished the oil lamp and stepped into darkness thicker than anything she had ever experienced. As she tried to settle into the state that produced light during meditation, panic welled up from depths she didn't recognize. The meditation hut was one thing; this underground void felt like being swallowed by the earth itself.

For several minutes, she stood frozen at the threshold, unable to summon even the faintest glow. The heat pressed in from all sides while fear dissolved her focus faster than she could rebuild it.

"I can't do this," she called out, her voice bouncing back from unseen stone walls.

"You can't do it," Venerable Thura agreed from somewhere outside the cave. "But consciousness can. Stop trying to generate light, and allow light to generate itself through you."

I'm afraid, she told the darkness silently. *And I'm miserable in this heat. But we can be frightened and uncomfortable together and still move forward.*

For the first hour, nothing changed. The familiar pattern repeated—panic rising as darkness pressed against her from all sides, her breathing becoming shallow in the oppressive air. But instead of fighting or fleeing, she held the fear like a crying child, neither pushing it away nor being consumed by it.

Her shirt clung to her back with sweat. The cave's heat felt like breathing through wet wool. Every instinct screamed at her to retreat, but she remained at the threshold, neither advancing nor retreating, simply being present with the overwhelming difficulty.

This is impossible, her mind whispered. *You're torturing yourself for nothing.*

Maybe, she replied to her own thoughts. *But I'm staying anyway.*

Slowly—so slowly she almost missed it—something began to shift, not in the external conditions, which remained brutally challenging, but in her relationship to them. The fear was still there, but it no longer felt like an enemy to be defeated. The heat was still oppressive, but it no longer seemed designed to drive her away. They were simply conditions, like weather, to be experienced rather than fought.

Another thirty minutes passed before she noticed the first change in her hands.

It began as warmth—not the external heat of the cave, but something generating from within her palms. At first, she thought it might be her circulation responding to stress. But the warmth had a different quality, more like the feeling she got when holding something precious, or the sensation in her chest during loving-kindness meditation.

Don't get excited, she warned herself, remembering how anticipation had killed previous glimmers of progress. *Just notice and stay present.*

The warmth spread slowly up her arms, taking another twenty minutes to reach her shoulders. It felt like liquid light moving through her bloodstream, but so subtle she had to keep checking whether she was imagining it. With the warmth came a strange sense of expansion, as if the boundaries of her body were becoming less definite.

Then, barely perceptible in the absolute darkness, she noticed her hands weren't completely invisible anymore.

The glow was so faint it was hardly there—like the afterglow behind closed eyelids after looking at a bright light. She had to look away and back again to convince herself it wasn't wishful thinking. Her palms held the barest suggestion of illumination, as if someone had turned a dimmer switch from zero to the first faint notch.

More, her ego whispered urgently. *Make it brighter. This is it—push harder now.*

The moment she tried to intensify the light through effort, it vanished completely, leaving her in total darkness again. Her heart sank like a stone.

But the warmth remained.

Ah, she understood suddenly. *Trying kills it. Allowing lets it grow.*

She spent another hour learning this delicate balance—not trying to create light, but also not being passive. It was more like tending a fragile flame, providing just enough attention to keep it alive without smothering it with effort.

The glow returned, faint as starlight, then gradually strengthened. After two more hours in the cave, she could make out the rough texture of the limestone walls around her. Not clearly—it was more like seeing by moonlight through fog—but enough to distinguish solid surfaces from empty space.

Each step deeper into the cave required her to maintain this impossible balance. Too much effort, and the light disappeared. Too little attention and it faded away. She had to stay right at the edge between caring and not caring, between trying and allowing.

Her clothes were soaked through with perspiration. Her legs shook with exhaustion from the constant tension between fear and acceptance. But step by careful step, she made her way deeper into the mountain, guided by light that seemed to come from love itself rather than her personal will.

When she finally reached the deepest chamber—a natural cathedral carved by water over millennia—the light around her was steady enough to reveal the crystalline formations on the walls. She sat in that sacred space for twenty minutes, not in triumph, but in profound humility at what consciousness could accomplish when it stopped trying to accomplish anything.

The journey back took another two hours. By the time she emerged, the sun was setting, and Venerable Thura was precisely where she had left him eight hours earlier, apparently unmoved despite the blazing heat.

"Fourth attempt," he said, noting her exhausted but radiant state. "Good persistence. Eight hours in the cave. Heat and fear have shown you that acceptance creates the conditions in which abilities can flourish, but maintaining them requires constant vigilance. You have passed the first test."

As Sarah walked back toward the monastery in the pale evening light, her legs still trembling from the ordeal, she understood that she had crossed more than a physical threshold. The light she had generated wasn't a supernatural power she had acquired—it was a natural capacity she had finally stopped preventing from expressing itself.

But the cave navigation was only the first of several increasingly challenging tests. Over the fourth week, Sarah learned to maintain luminosity while helping with monastery maintenance, during village healing sessions where she assisted other practition-ers, and even while sleeping—waking to find her small room filled with gentle golden light that had apparently been sustaining itself throughout the night.

"Light generation affects your entire life, not just formal prac-tice periods," Venerable Thura explained, when Sarah described waking to find herself glowing. "Advanced practitioners live in constant recognition of their luminous nature. The ability becomes as natural as breathing, as automatic as heartbeat."

The training culminated in what Venerable Thura called "demonstration teaching"—using light generation to help village children who were afraid of darkness. Sarah spent an evening with twelve children, aged five to ten, teaching them that consciousness itself is luminous and that they can learn to access their own inner light when external illumination is unavailable.

"Watch carefully," she said to the assembled children, speaking through Min Thant's translation. "Light doesn't come from outside us—it comes from the love inside us."

As she allowed golden radiance to fill the darkened room, the children's faces transformed from anxiety to wonder. Several began laughing with delight, reaching toward the luminosity as though it were something they could touch and hold.

"Can we learn to do that?" asked a seven-year-old girl whose fear of nighttime had been troubling her family.

"Everyone can learn," Sarah replied, understanding with certainty that was indeed the case. "Light is what you are, not something you have to get from somewhere else."

By the end of the teaching session, three of the children had managed to produce faint glows from their hands, their natural openness allowing rapid development that sometimes took adults months to achieve. Sarah watched their excitement with profound gratitude for having discovered abilities that could serve the well-being of others rather than just her own spiritual development.

"Individual abilities that serve only personal benefit represent incomplete understanding," Venerable Thura observed as they walked back to the monastery compound. "True spiritual development naturally flows toward helping others recognize their own unlimited nature. The light you can generate is consciousness teaching itself about its own creative potential."

As they prepared to begin the second level of training—telepathy, or *cetopariyañāṇa*—Sarah realized that light generation had fundamentally transformed her understanding of the relationship between individual consciousness and universal creative power. The abilities she was developing belonged not to "Sarah the academic," but to awareness itself, temporarily expressing its unlimited creativity through the form that appeared as an individual practitioner but had never actually been separate from the whole.

"Tomorrow we begin the second level," Venerable Thura announced as they concluded their final light generation evaluation session. "Direct awareness of mind streams. But first, you must understand: the light you can now generate externally has always been shining as the luminosity of your own awareness. The minds you will learn to read are not separate from the consciousness that is reading them."

Sarah experienced the familiar blend of excitement and apprehension, which was becoming typical at each new training level. Every stage of growth offered not only new skills but also a deeper breakdown of the boundaries that had once defined her identity and perception of reality.

Tomorrow, she would begin discovering whether the boundaries between individual minds were as illusory as the boundaries between consciousness and luminosity had proven to be.

The academic who had studied consciousness from the outside was becoming consciousness itself, systematically awakening to capacities that revealed the ultimate nature of what she had always been, but had temporarily forgotten, in the beautiful game of spiritual seeking that always ended with recognition of what had never actually been lost.

But tonight, as she sat in her small room filled with the gentle golden light that now accompanied her everywhere, Sarah understood that even the most extraordinary abilities were simply expressions of the love that was consciousness knowing itself through countless forms, each awakening serving the awakening of all.

The light bearer was ready to become the mind reader, and the mind reader would eventually become the time walker. Each level revealed deeper aspects of the one awareness that appeared as all experiences, all abilities, and all apparent individuals, learning to recognize their shared luminous nature.

CHAPTER 5: THE MIND READER

Second Level Training: Telepathy (Cetopariyañāṇa)

Sarah's fifth week at the monastery began with her legs finally accepting lotus position without active rebellion, a small victory that felt monumental after days of negotiating with joints designed for chairs rather than floors. The morning mist clung to ancient stones like incense made visible, and for the first time since arriving, she walked to the meditation hall without dreading the next hour of seated endurance.

The transformation in her relationship with physical discomfort surprised her. Where once her ankles had locked in protest and her knees had refused to cooperate, now her body seemed to have learned the monastery's language of patient acceptance. The aching had become familiar, like background music that no longer demanded conscious attention. Her Western anatomy was slowly adapting to arrangements that had served contemplatives for millennia.

The pre-dawn air carried scents of jasmine and wood smoke, sounds of monastery life beginning its daily rhythm—distant temple bells marking group meditation time, soft footfalls of robed figures moving between buildings with unhurried purpose, the gentle percussion of wooden bowls being arranged for morning meals by monks who had transformed even the simplest tasks into forms of meditation.

Sarah had learned to move with their measured pace, each step deliberate rather than efficient, as though walking itself were a form of prayer requiring the same attention she had once reserved for complex academic problems. The monastery's rhythm was rewiring her nervous system, teaching her body to find grace in slowness, meaning in simplicity.

Her sleep had changed too. The dreams that had once churned with academic anxieties and professional concerns had given way to landscapes of startling clarity—vast spaces where thoughts arose and dissolved like clouds in an infinite sky, conversations with teachers who spoke in languages she didn't recognize but somehow understood completely, visions of light streaming from her hands in ways that felt both impossible and inevitable.

This morning felt different from the others. There was anticipation in the air, a sense that she was approaching some threshold that would fundamentally alter her understanding of what human consciousness could accomplish. The feeling had been building for days, like pressure gathering before a storm, though what might break open remained mysteriously beyond her ability to anticipate.

Venerable Thura waited in the center of the hall, but today something was different. Instead of taking his usual position facing the assembled monks, he sat at the room's back, beside a cushion clearly intended for her. The arrangement felt intimate, almost conspiratorial, as though she were being invited into a tutorial that existed separately from the community's regular practice.

The other monks had already settled into their morning meditation, forty figures arranged in perfect rows. Their collective stillness created a field of concentration so refined that Sarah could feel it pressing against her awareness like a gentle tide. The meditation hall hummed with focused intention, each practitioner contributing to an atmosphere that made her usual mental chatter seem deafeningly loud by comparison.

She had come to recognize the subtle variations in their practice—the way Min Thant's attention moved like water finding its natural level, the elderly monk whose arthritic discomfort dissolved into something approaching bliss through sheer acceptance, the young novice who still wrestled with homesickness but was learning to hold even that struggle with compassion. Each mind contributed its own note to a symphony of consciousness exploring itself through sustained inquiry.

"Today we begin *cetopariyañāṇa*," Venerable Thura said as she settled beside him, voice pitched low enough that the other monks couldn't overhear. His presence radiated the same quality of stillness that characterized the Buddha statue behind him, but with a warmth that suggested consciousness awakened rather than consciousness carved from stone. "Awareness of mind streams. The second foundation of mindfulness in our tradition."

Sarah nodded, though Pali terms still felt like artifacts from a museum she was allowed to visit but not inhabit. She had read extensively about the four foundations of mindfulness—body awareness, feeling sensations, mental formations, and investigation of phenomena—but experiencing them directly required a different kind of literacy than her academic training had provided. The gap between conceptual knowledge and lived understanding had become a chasm she was only beginning to learn how to cross.

Her academic mind immediately began cataloguing what she knew about *cetopariyañāṇa* from scholarly sources: the systematic observation of mental processes described in the *Visuddhimagga*, neurological studies showing how sustained attention to cognitive activity altered default mode network functioning, phenomenological accounts from experienced practitioners across various contemplative traditions. But even as this information arose, she recognized it as the very kind of mental activity the practice was designed to observe rather than indulge.

"The mind you are about to observe," Venerable Thura

continued, seeming to read her academic reflexes with uncanny accuracy, "is not an object to be studied but the subject doing the studying. This investigation will reveal that the observer and the observed are both appearances within something far more fundamental than either."

His words carried implications that made her scholarly training seem suddenly inadequate. She had spent years researching consciousness as though it were something she could examine from the outside, like a specimen under a microscope. But what if consciousness was the microscope, the specimen, and the scientist all simultaneously?

"Close your eyes," Venerable Thura instructed, his voice carrying the patience of someone who had guided countless students through this same threshold between theoretical understanding and direct recognition. "But instead of following your breath, turn attention toward the mind itself. Notice thoughts as they arise and pass away. See if you can observe the space between which thinking occurs."

Sarah obeyed, settling into the stillness that was becoming familiar territory. Her breath found its natural rhythm while attention turned inward, seeking the thoughts that usually dominated every waking moment. But in the focusing silence, her mind seemed strangely empty, as though thoughts were shy creatures hiding when directly observed.

This was different from her usual struggles with meditation. Instead of the familiar tornado of analysis, planning, and worry that typically characterized her attempts at contemplative practice, she found herself in a space of unusual quiet. It was as though four weeks of sustained practice had finally worn down the mental habits that had resisted every previous effort at sustained attention.

The silence wasn't empty, though. It had texture, depth, a quality of aliveness that suggested vast activity occurring below the threshold of ordinary awareness. Like looking into deep water where movement was visible but the creatures creating it remained hidden, her consciousness seemed to be teeming with processes that operated beyond the reach of surface thinking.

"There's nothing there," she whispered after several minutes of searching for mental activity that refused to appear.

"Look more carefully," Venerable Thura suggested, his words seeming to arise from the silence itself rather than breaking it. "Not for thoughts, but for the awareness that knows whether thoughts are present or absent. What is it that recognizes emptiness when emptiness appears?"

The instruction redirected her attention with surgical precision. Instead of seeking mental content, she began observing the consciousness that noticed mental content—or its absence. It was like discovering she had been looking at her hand while missing the eye doing the looking, or studying waves while remaining blind to the ocean that created them.

This shift in perspective was disorienting. Her entire academic career had been built on the assumption that consciousness was something she possessed and could therefore study objectively. But now she was discovering that consciousness wasn't a possession at all—it was the very capacity for possessing, knowing, experiencing anything whatsoever. It was like a flashlight trying to illuminate itself, or an eye attempting to see its own seeing.

"I can sense... spaciousness," she said tentatively, voice barely audible in the hall's concentrated quiet. "Like a clear sky that could hold clouds but doesn't need to. It's aware, but not of anything in particular."

"Yes. And what is the nature of this awareness? Does it have boundaries? Does it belong to anyone in particular? Can you find where it begins or ends?"

The questions guided her investigation deeper into territory she had never explored despite years of consciousness research. The more carefully she examined the awareness that was aware of thoughts, the less personal it seemed. It felt vast, open, completely without characteristics that would mark it as belonging to "Dr. Sarah Chen" rather than consciousness itself.

It was like discovering that what she had always assumed to be her private inner world was actually a shared space —a universal field of knowing in which all experiences arose and dissolved. The boundaries she had taken for granted—between inner and outer, self and other, knower and known—began to feel arbitrary, like lines drawn on water that appeared real until examined closely.

"It doesn't feel like mine," she admitted, surprised by the recognition. "It's more like... space itself. Present but empty. Knowing but without knowledge. It seems to have no center, no edges, no characteristics that would make it personal."

"This is *cetopariyañāṇa*," Venerable Thura said, satisfaction evident in his tone. "The recognition that the individual mind is an appearance within universal awareness. What you call 'your consciousness' is actually consciousness itself, temporarily appearing to be personal."

The words struck her like lightning, revealing a landscape that had always been present in darkness. For weeks, she had been trying to develop her consciousness, improve her meditation, and achieve higher states of awareness. But if consciousness wasn't personal in the first place, what exactly was she trying to develop?

Sarah's hands trembled as the recognition settled deeper. She could feel Min Thant's approach before she saw him, his concern radiating like heat from a fire. The telepathic sensitivity that had seemed impossible just minutes ago was already becoming involuntary and unstoppable.

"The first time is overwhelming," he said gently, settling beside her. "I spent three days after my first contact convinced I was losing my mind."

"How do you function," she whispered, "when you can sense everyone's thoughts? When privacy is revealed as an illusion?"

"You learn that what feels like invasion is actually recognition," Min Thant replied. "The thoughts you perceive were never separate from your own awareness anyway."

"Now," Venerable Thura continued, "extend this awareness

beyond the boundaries you assume separate you from others. Let consciousness recognize itself everywhere it appears."

"I don't understand how to do that."

"You don't do it. You simply stop preventing it. Like removing walls from a room and discovering the space was never actually confined."

Sarah attempted to follow the instructions, though it felt like being asked to see with someone else's eyes. She allowed her awareness to expand beyond what she normally considered the borders of her experience, letting attention extend into the space around her body, beyond the cushion, into the meditation hall itself.

At first, nothing happened except a vague sense of diffusion, as though her attention were spreading too thin to be useful. But gradually, something extraordinary began to occur. The boundaries between inside and outside, between her consciousness and the hall's space, began to feel arbitrary rather than absolute.

And then, without warning, thoughts appeared in her awareness that carried a distinctly unfamiliar quality.

The new student progresses quickly. Too quickly perhaps. Western minds often mistake initial openings for final understanding.

The thoughts arose with the same immediacy as her own mental activity, but something about their tone, their content, their very texture felt foreign. Sarah's eyes snapped open to find Venerable Thura watching her with an expression of patient curiosity, his dark eyes holding depths that seemed to reflect her own surprise.

"Did you just think about my progress being too quick?" she asked, voice barely above a whisper.

His eyebrows rose slightly—the first time she had seen him display anything resembling surprise. "Describe what you experienced."

"I heard... or felt... thoughts that didn't seem to be mine. Something about Western minds mistaking initial openings for final understanding." Sarah studied his face intently. "Were those your thoughts?"

"What do you think?"

The question carried more weight than simple curiosity. Sarah closed her eyes again, returning attention to the expanded awareness she had discovered. This time, the foreign thoughts came more clearly, accompanied by what could only be described as emotional undertones that had nothing to do with her current feelings.

She has a natural ability but lacks a foundation. The ego will try to claim these experiences as personal achievement. Must proceed carefully to avoid spiritual materialism.

"You're concerned that I'll become attached to unusual experiences," Sarah said aloud, opening her eyes to meet his gaze. "You're thinking about what you call 'spiritual materialism'—using awakening as another form of ego enhancement."

Venerable Thura's expression shifted from curiosity to something approaching amazement. "In thirty years of teaching, I have never seen *cetopariyañāṇa* develop so rapidly." He paused, studying her with renewed interest. "How clearly can you perceive these mental streams?"

"It's like..." Sarah searched for an adequate description. "Like tuning a radio and discovering I can pick up multiple stations simultaneously. Your thoughts feel more structured, more peaceful than mine. There's less urgency, less grasping."

"Try extending further," he suggested. "Can you sense the mental activity of others in the hall?"

Sarah closed her eyes again, allowing awareness to expand throughout the meditation space. At first, the thirty monks seemed like islands of silence, their concentration too deep for surface thoughts to penetrate. But as her sensitivity increased, she began to detect subtle currents of mental activity even in their profound stillness.

From Min Thant, seated three rows ahead: gentle concern

about whether he was breathing too loudly, mixed with gratitude for the morning's teaching.

From an elderly monk near the wall: physical discomfort in arthritic knees, held within such acceptance that pain became almost indistinguishable from peace.

From a young novice close to her own age: homesickness for his village, combined with determination to remain present despite emotional difficulty.

Each mind carried its own signature, its own quality of attention and concern, yet all seemed to be variations on the same underlying consciousness she had discovered in herself. Like instruments in an orchestra, each is unique but participates in a symphony too vast for any individual player to fully comprehend.

"This is impossible," Sarah whispered, opening her eyes to find Venerable Thura regarding her with an expression she couldn't interpret.

"Why impossible?"

"Because telepathy isn't real. It violates every principle of neuroscience, every understanding of how consciousness operates. Minds are generated by individual brains. They can't... overlap like this."

"And yet," Venerable Thura observed mildly, as though students routinely demonstrated impossible abilities during his teachings, "you just demonstrated precisely such overlap."

Sarah felt the familiar tension between her direct experience and her conceptual framework, which had been building since she arrived. Her academic training insisted that what she was experiencing must be imagination, projection, or coincidence—anything except an accurate perception of other minds. But the accuracy, the specificity, and the alien quality of the thoughts she was receiving pointed to something far beyond wishful thinking.

"How is this possible?" she asked.

"Perhaps the question assumes something incorrect," he responded. "You ask how individual minds can overlap, but what if individual minds are conceptual constructions rather than actual realities?"

The suggestion hit her like cold water. "You're saying consciousness isn't personal?"

"I'm suggesting you investigate for yourself. When you examine this awareness that can apparently perceive multiple mental streams, does it seem to belong to any particular person? Or does it seem more like space itself—present everywhere, bounded nowhere, capable of holding any content without being defined by what it contains?"

Sarah turned attention back to the expanded awareness she had discovered, examining its qualities with investigative precision, her scientific training having developed. The consciousness that could perceive her thoughts, Venerable Thura's thoughts, and the mental activity of distant monks didn't feel like "her" consciousness extended outward. It felt more like universal consciousness temporarily appearing to be personal, like the sky appearing to be owned by whatever landscape lay beneath it.

"It feels like..." She struggled for an adequate metaphor. "Like I've been assuming I was a separate wave, only to discover I'm actually the ocean appearing as waves."

"Yes," Venerable Thura said with obvious satisfaction. "This is the deeper recognition *cetopariyañāṇa* reveals. What we call telepathy is simply consciousness recognizing itself across apparent boundaries."

Over the following days, Sarah's awareness of other minds grew with alarming speed, questioning all her previous beliefs about individual consciousness.

As her telepathic sensitivity deepened with startling speed, Sarah was haunted by thoughts of Elena Martinez. If she had possessed this ability during her student's dissertation defense, she might have perceived the mounting terror beneath Elena's academic composure before it exploded into public breakdown. Instead of watching helplessly as Elena's intellectual defenses cracked under examination pressure, Sarah could have sensed the psychological storm gathering and intervened before it became irreversible. Elena's mind had been screaming for help while her mouth spoke theoretical frameworks about healing trauma. With telepathic awareness, Sarah might have heard that silent cry and provided real support instead of standing by with useless academic platitudes while her student's sanity disintegrated before her.

During meals, she found herself overwhelmed by the emotional undertones of forty monks eating in silence—their gratitude for simple nourishment, their homesickness for families left behind in service of awakening, their varied relationships with monastic discipline creating a symphony of feeling that threatened to dissolve her sense of individual boundaries entirely.

The experience was like suddenly being able to hear radio frequencies that had always been broadcasting but which her receiver had never been calibrated to detect. Each mind carried its own emotional signature, its own quality of attention and concern. Yet, all seemed to be variations on the same underlying consciousness she had discovered in herself during *cetopariyañāṇa* practice.

During walking meditation, she could perceive the quality of attention each practitioner brought to their steps—some mechanical and distracted, some devotional and surrendered, some analytical and self-conscious, all variations on the theme of consciousness exploring its own nature through the simple act of mindful movement. The young novice still struggled with restlessness that made each step feel like an eternity. The elderly monk had found such peace in slowness that walking became a form of prayer. Min Thant moved with the fluid grace of someone who had discovered that the walker and the walking were not separate activities.

But perhaps most disturbing was her growing ability to sense the academic skepticism that arose in visiting scholars and researchers who occasionally came to observe monastery life. Their mental activity felt familiar because it mirrored her own pre-arrival consciousness—analytical, categorizing, maintaining careful distance from the very experiences they claimed to be studying. She could feel their discomfort with anything that challenged materialist assumptions, their need to explain away rather than investigate phenomena that didn't fit conventional paradigms.

The ability was extraordinary and terrifying in equal measure. Sarah had spent her career studying consciousness as an object of investigation, something that could be measured, categorized, and understood through empirical methodology. But now consciousness was revealing itself as the subject that had been doing the investigating all along, the very field within which all objects arose and were known.

The implications staggered her understanding of mind, identity, and human experience. If consciousness was universal rather than individual, if telepathic perception was simply awareness recognizing itself across apparent boundaries, if the sense of being a separate self was a kind of optical illusion created by identification with thought processes—then everything she had been taught about human nature required complete revision.

But it was during a solo meditation session in her quarters that the real test came, challenging her growing abilities in ways that would either confirm or demolish everything she was beginning to understand about the nature of consciousness.

As afternoon light slanted through her window, creating patterns that shifted with each breath of wind through the garden outside, Sarah sat practicing the expanded awareness Venerable Thura had introduced. The heat of the day had reached its peak, making the air thick and still, but inside her simple room, something approaching coolness persisted in the shadows cast by wooden shutters.

Her attention had settled into what was becoming a familiar sense of boundless space—the recognition that awareness itself had no borders, no center, no characteristics that would make it personal property rather than universal presence. In this expanded state, the boundaries between her consciousness and the world around her felt arbitrary, like rainbows that appeared solid until examined closely.

It was in this state of openness that sudden distress flooded her awareness—not her own, but someone else's fear and confusion so intense it felt like drowning in another person's nightmare. The emotional storm struck without warning, carrying with it a desperation so profound it made her chest constrict until breathing became difficult.

The distress was accompanied by images that arose in her awareness with startling clarity: a young woman, perhaps twenty-five, sitting alone in a sparse room that bore some resemblance to Sarah's own quarters but felt fundamentally different. Where the monastery radiated peace and acceptance, this space carried the sterile atmosphere of institutional care, a kind of environment designed to focus on getting things done rather than promoting healing.

Without a conscious decision, Sarah found her awareness drawn toward this distant suffering like iron filings toward a magnet; her consciousness extended across what might have been vast distances to touch this stranger's pain. The images became clearer, more detailed, as though she were adjusting the focus on some impossible telescope that could peer into lives rather than landscapes.

A hospital room. Medical equipment humming with electronic vigilance. The woman was a patient, not a guest, and her distress centered on news she had recently received about her condition. The diagnosis had been delivered with the clinical precision that medical professionals used to distance themselves from emotional impact: malignant, aggressive, terminal. Six months, perhaps less, depending on how well she responded to treatments that offered hope for extension rather than cure.

Terminal diagnosis. Six months. The words arose in Sarah's awareness with crushing clarity, carrying emotional weight that seemed to compress her chest until breathing became difficult. The woman's despair wasn't just about death—it was about incompleteness, about dreams that would remain unrealized, about the cruel arbitrariness of having consciousness awakened to its own mortality just as life was beginning to feel meaningful.

Sarah opened her eyes, gasping as though she had been holding her breath underwater for longer than her lungs could sustain. The connection severed immediately, leaving her alone in her monastery quarters with afternoon light still painting peaceful patterns on the wooden floor. But the woman's despair lingered in her awareness like smoke after fire, impossible to dismiss as imagination or projection.

The experience left her shaking with questions that challenged everything she thought she understood about the nature of human consciousness. Had she genuinely perceived someone thousands of miles away, or was her mind creating elaborate fantasies to explain unusual mental states? Could consciousness actually extend beyond the brain that generated it, or was she experiencing some kind of psychological phenomenon that neuroscience could explain through conventional mechanisms?

She found Venerable Thura tending the lotus garden behind the main hall, arranging flowers with the same meticulous attention he brought to everything else. His hands moved among the blooms with surgical precision, each placement serving both aesthetic and practical purposes, creating arrangements that seemed to emerge from natural law rather than human design.

The garden itself was a study in impermanence, one that was embraced rather than fought. Lotus blossoms in various stages of opening and closing demonstrated the Buddhist teaching about the inevitability of change. At the same time, the carefully maintained pond reflected light in patterns that shifted moment by moment. It was here that many of the monastery's most profound teachings occurred, not through formal instruction but through the simple act of observing natural processes with sustained attention.

"Venerable Thura," she said, approaching carefully so as not to disturb his concentration. The elderly teacher's awareness seemed to encompass multiple activities simultaneously—tending to the flowers, monitoring the afternoon light, and remaining alert to whatever students at various stages of development might need instruction. "I think I connected with someone who wasn't here. Someone in distress."

He looked up from the flowers he was arranging, his expression growing more serious as she described the hospital room, the young woman, the terminal diagnosis that had generated such overwhelming despair. Venerable Thura listened without interruption, his attention completely focused on her account while his hands continued their delicate work among the lotus stems.

His capacity for simultaneous attention amazed her. Where Western culture emphasized the value of focused concentration on single tasks, contemplative training appeared to cultivate awareness that could maintain precision in multiple streams of activity without losing focus in any particular area. It was like watching someone conduct an orchestra while also playing first violin.

"You perceived someone beyond the physical boundaries of this monastery," he said when she finished, setting down his gardening tools and giving her his complete attention. "This is advanced *cetopariyañāṇa*. But such sensitivity brings responsibility that cannot be ignored or abandoned once it has been awakened."

"What kind of responsibility?"

Venerable Thura gestured for her to sit on the stone bench that overlooked the pond, where afternoon light created patterns of illumination that seemed to dance with each ripple on the water's surface. "When consciousness recognizes its universal nature, it naturally responds to suffering wherever it appears. You may find yourself drawn to offer assistance in ways that transcend conventional limitations of space, time, and physical proximity."

The implications were staggering. Sarah had been trained to think of helping others in terms of direct action—research that led to therapeutic applications, teaching that conveyed useful knowledge, and charitable activities that addressed material needs. However, the idea of providing aid via pure consciousness over great distances to people she had never met challenged every preconception about how helpful actions take place.

"How can I help someone I've never met? Someone who might be thousands of miles away?"

Venerable Thura studied her with the same careful attention he brought to arranging flowers, as though her question revealed exactly where her understanding needed to develop next. "The same consciousness that allowed you to perceive her distress can extend healing and comfort across any distance. But this requires understanding what you truly are and what you're truly capable of accomplishing through intention purified of personal agenda."

"I don't understand what you mean."

"Tonight, during evening meditation, return your attention to this young woman. But instead of simply observing her suffering, suffuse her with your loving kindness—allow the love that is your deepest nature to extend toward her. See what happens when consciousness offers comfort to itself across apparent separation. Discover whether the boundaries you assume exist between beings are as solid as they appear."

That evening, as monastery bells called the community to final practice, Sarah was sitting in her room, her hands shaking and her heart pounding. She couldn't help but feel the weight of what she was about to do. The possibility of actually helping someone through pure intention felt simultaneously thrilling and terrifying, like standing at the edge of a cliff where jumping might mean flying or falling, depending on the laws of physics she didn't understand.

Everything in her scientific training insisted such ideas were nonsense, elaborate fantasies generated by meditative states that altered brain chemistry in ways that created convincing hallucinations. But five weeks of direct experience had already shattered most of her certainties about the nature of reality, leaving her open to possibilities that would have seemed absurd during her previous life as a consciousness researcher.

The monastery night settled around her with its characteristic depth, sounds of the community ending their day with the same unhurried attention they brought to all activities. Somewhere in the compound, monks were completing their final prayers, arranging their simple quarters for sleep, and reviewing the day's insights in ways that transformed even rest into a contemplative practice.

She closed her eyes and allowed awareness to expand in a way that had become natural, seeking the emotional signature she had encountered that afternoon. At first, she found only silence and space, the vast field of consciousness within which all experience arose and dissolved. Then, gradually, like tuning a radio to a distant station, the young woman's presence became perceptible again.

She was still in the hospital room, stuck in that clean, clinical space where everything seemed to focus more on getting things done than actually making her feel better, but her emotional state had shifted dramatically. Instead of overwhelming despair, Sarah sensed a quality of quiet contemplation, as though the woman were having thoughts that surprised her with their peacefulness. And beneath the surface thinking, something even more subtle: a sense of being held, of not being as alone as circumstances suggested.

Following Venerable Thura's instruction, Sarah allowed love to extend across whatever distance separated them. Not sentimental emotion or sympathetic pity, but the unconditioned care that seemed to be consciousness's natural response to its own appearances. She held the woman in awareness the way space holds stars—completely, effortlessly, without agenda or attachment to outcomes, offering presence that asked nothing in return.

The love that flowed through her felt impersonal in the most beautiful sense—not generated by Sarah Chen's personality or emotional history, but arising from the same source that made compassion possible throughout the universe. It was like becoming a conduit for something infinitely larger than individual identity, a force that existed wherever consciousness recognized itself in apparent distress.

For perhaps an hour, Sarah maintained this connection, offering silent presence to someone she had never met but who felt as familiar as her own heartbeat. The experience challenged assumptions about the boundaries between self and other, helper and helped, here and there. If consciousness were universal, helping this woman was like helping herself, offering comfort to the same awareness sitting in a monastery thousands of miles away.

When she finally opened her eyes, monastery night had settled completely around her. Still, something fundamental had shifted in her understanding of what it meant to be conscious, to be helpful, to be alive in a universe where separation might be the primary illusion that consciousness created to experience love as a relationship rather than simple self-recognition.

The next morning, Venerable Thura found her in the meditation hall before dawn practice began, sitting in the same spot where their lessons had started weeks earlier. His presence radiated the quiet satisfaction of a teacher whose student had successfully navigated a particularly challenging threshold. However, his expression remained neutral enough to avoid creating pride or attachment to spiritual accomplishment.

"The young woman," he said without preamble, settling beside her with his characteristic grace. "How was she when you connected last night?"

"Better," Sarah replied, still amazed by what had occurred and uncertain how to integrate the experience into any framework that made rational sense. "Calmer. Like she was receiving comfort from somewhere she couldn't identify. There was still sadness about her diagnosis, but it was held within something larger than despair."

"And how do you understand what occurred?"

Sarah considered the question carefully, feeling her way toward language adequate for experiences that seemed to exist beyond conventional categories of helper and helped, here and there, self and other. "I think consciousness offered healing to itself across the appearance of separation. Like the ocean soothing waves that had forgotten they were ocean."

Venerable Thura smiled with the satisfaction of someone whose most promising student had just grasped a lesson that usually required years to integrate, someone whose capacity for learning had exceeded even optimistic expectations.

"You are ready," he said, his words carrying the weight of formal transmission, "to learn what consciousness can do when it stops pretending to be limited by individual identity."

Sarah felt a shift inside her at his words, like a door opening to vast realms she never knew existed. Her academic view of consciousness as a brain-generated phenomenon was dissolving, replaced by a direct awareness that consciousness is the foundation of all experience. The implications were enormous, not just for her personal growth but for everything she believed about human potential and the nature of reality.

CHAPTER 6: THE TIME WALKER

THIRD LEVEL TRAINING: TIME PERCEPTION (KĀLAÑĀṆA)

Telepathic abilities had already dissolved Sarah's assumptions about the boundaries between individual minds. Now she was about to discover whether consciousness could transcend temporal limitations as easily as it had transcended the apparent separation between different mental streams.

Consciousness was preparing to discover that time itself was a modification of awareness that had never actually been bound by the limitations it appeared to experience through identification with particular moments, memories, and anticipated futures.

Week One: The Nature of Time Perception

The third level of training began in the limestone cave where Sarah had first learned to access historical memories embedded in the monastery's stone walls. Still, now, after months of systematic consciousness development, the cave felt different—not just a meditation space, but a portal into dimensions of awareness that existed outside conventional temporal boundaries.

The early morning mist clung to the mountain peaks as Sarah followed Venerable Thura along the narrow path that led to the cave entrance, her footsteps echoing the countless pilgrims who had made this same journey over eight centuries of spiritual transmission. The cave system extended deep into the mountain, with chambers that had been used for intensive meditation practice since the monastery's founding by the Indian master who had first brought these consciousness development teachings to Myanmar.

"Time is the most persistent illusion maintained by ordinary consciousness," Venerable Thura explained as they settled into meditation posture in the cave's natural alcove, his voice carrying the same quality of depth and precision that had characterized all his teaching. "Light generation demonstrated that consciousness and energy are unified. Telepathy revealed that individual minds are modifications of universal awareness. Time perception training will show you that past, present, and future are mental constructs rather than objective realities."

Sarah felt her academic background engaging with these concepts in ways that were both helpful and limiting. Her university studies had included extensive work on the phenomenology of temporal experience—how consciousness creates the sense of linear time through memory, attention, and anticipation. But the training she was about to receive would go far beyond philosophical understanding into direct manipulation of time perception itself.

"From the perspective of awakened consciousness, all moments exist simultaneously," Venerable Thura continued, his words seeming to resonate through the cave's ancient stone walls. "What you call 'past' is consciousness appearing as memory. What you call 'future' is consciousness appearing as possibility. What you call 'present' is consciousness recognizing its own timeless nature."

The instruction that followed made Sarah question everything she knew about the nature of temporal experience. Instead of viewing time as a linear flow carrying her forward from past through present toward future, she was guided to recognize time as a space-like dimension that consciousness could navigate in any direction when properly trained.

"Time is like a vast library," Venerable Thura taught during their first session. "From within any particular book, the story seems to unfold sequentially page by page. But the entire library exists simultaneously, and a consciousness that learns to step outside identification with particular narratives can access any volume, any chapter, any page when properly trained."

The initial exercises involved learning to perceive what Venerable Thura called "temporal impressions"—emotional and energetic residues left by previous events that remained accessible to sufficiently refined awareness. The limestone cave, having been used for intensive meditation practice for over eight centuries, provided an ideal training environment because the accumulated spiritual energy created what felt like temporal layers that could be detected through expanded perception.

"Rest in the same awareness you discovered during telepathy training," Venerable Thura instructed as Sarah settled into meditation posture on the smooth stone floor. "But instead of reaching toward other minds, allow your attention to sink backward into the historical information embedded in this space."

At first, Sarah experienced nothing beyond the familiar qualities of meditative absorption—the settling of mental activity, the expansion of awareness, the dissolution of ordinary subject-object boundaries. But gradually, as she learned to maintain the open, receptive quality of attention that had served her telepathic development, subtle impressions began arising that felt distinctly different from products of imagination.

Images of the cave, which countless previous practitioners have used over centuries. Emotional resonances of profound meditative states achieved by generations of monks who had sought awakening in this same space. The accumulated energetic imprint of thousands of hours of intensive spiritual practice created what felt like temporal layers that could be accessed through a tuned, concentrated mind.

"What you are perceiving," Venerable Thura explained when Sarah described these impressions during their first evaluation, "represents the first level of time perception—sensing the historical information that remains embedded in physical locations due to the intensity of events that occurred there. Every place carries temporal resonance that can be accessed by consciousness tuned to the right frequency."

The impressions became more vivid as her sensitivity developed. She could perceive what felt like different historical periods overlapping in the same physical space—the cave during its early years when Indian masters first established meditation practices there, periods of political turmoil when monks had hidden sacred texts within the cave's deeper chambers, times of renewal when new generations of teachers had revitalized contemplative training using methods refined through centuries of accumulated wisdom.

Over the first week, Sarah learned to distinguish between different types of historical information available through expanded time perception. Some impressions came through what felt like emotional resonance—the accumulated feeling-tones of joy, suffering, dedication, and awakening that had been experienced in the cave. Others came as more specific imagery—visual impressions of how the space had been used, who had practiced there, what kinds of spiritual experiences had unfolded over time.

"The cave serves as an excellent training ground because limestone itself has absorptive properties that retain temporal impressions more clearly than other materials," Venerable Thura explained during one of their sessions, where Sarah had successfully accessed what appeared to be historically accurate information about the cave's use over the previous century. "But advanced practitioners can access historical information from any location, and eventually even from objects that have been present during significant events."

The training also revealed how time perception operated according to principles that challenged conventional understanding of causation and information storage. Rather than accessing data that was somehow "recorded" in physical matter, Sarah was learning to recognize that all temporal experience existed simultaneously within consciousness, becoming accessible when awareness expanded beyond identification with particular moments or linear sequences.

"Time is like a movie film," Venerable Thura taught during a session where Sarah had successfully accessed memories from multiple historical periods within the same meditation sitting. "From within the movie, events appear to unfold sequentially. But the entire film exists as a complete unit that can be viewed from any point when consciousness steps outside linear identification with particular frames."

More significantly, she was beginning to understand that linear time was indeed a construct rather than an absolute reality —when consciousness shifted into sufficiently expanded awareness, past and present seemed to exist simultaneously rather than sequentially, accessible through attention that was no longer confined to identification with particular temporal positions.

"This training serves multiple purposes," Venerable Thura said during her first evaluation session. "Practically, it develops your ability to gather information that can serve diagnostic and healing purposes when working with individuals or communities carrying unresolved historical trauma. Philosophically, it demonstrates the fluid nature of temporal experience. But most importantly, it prepares consciousness for the recognition that what you call 'your life' is simply one temporary modification of awareness that has never actually been born and will never actually die."

Week Two: Personal Timeline Exploration and Past-Life Integration

The second week of time perception training involved what Venerable Thura called "personal temporal healing"—using expanded temporal awareness to identify and resolve psychological patterns rooted in past experiences, including what appeared to be past-life memories that influenced current personality dynamics and behavioral patterns.

"Most psychological suffering is temporal in nature," he explained as they began this phase of training in the deeper chambers of the cave system, where the limestone formations created natural sound amplification that enhanced the meditative states necessary for accessing distant temporal experiences. "Traumatic experiences create fixation points in consciousness that continue generating emotional disturbance long after the original events have passed. Advanced time perception allows healing at the temporal source rather than just managing present-moment symptoms."

Sarah's first experience with personal temporal healing was profound and disconcerting, challenging her beliefs about identity and the link between current patterns and influences from previous incarnations.

Under Venerable Thura's guidance, she learned to trace her persistent academic perfectionism back through what felt like a sequence of previous lifetimes where intellectual achievement had been either her means of survival or the cause of her persecution. The technique involved maintaining expanded temporal awareness while following emotional and psychological patterns backward through time until their origins became apparent.

The most vivid regression revealed what appeared to be a life as a female scholar in 12th-century Tibet, where her exceptional memory and analytical abilities had gained her access to rare manuscripts and recognition within monastic intellectual circles. But the same capabilities that had brought success had also created jealousy among male monastics who eventually orchestrated her exile from the monastery where she had spent most of her adult life.

"This feels incredibly real," Sarah reported during the session, her voice carrying amazement at the detail and emotional authenticity of what she was experiencing. "I can see the manuscript library, smell the yak butter lamps, feel the cold mountain air. But how can I know whether I'm accessing actual past-life memories or creating elaborate fantasies based on my current psychological patterns and knowledge of Tibetan Buddhism?"

"Excellent question," Venerable Thura replied with appreciation for her discriminating awareness. "The literal accuracy of past-life memories is less important than their therapeutic value for understanding and resolving current psychological patterns. Whether these impressions represent actual historical events or symbolic representations of psychological dynamics, they provide access to the temporal origins of present-moment suffering."

The past-life exploration revealed how her current relationship with intellectual achievement carried emotional patterns of both ambition and anxiety that seemed to originate from lifetimes where learning had been simultaneously her greatest strength and most dangerous vulnerability. Her academic perfectionism wasn't simply a personality quirk, but appeared to be a defensive strategy developed across multiple incarnations where intellectual competence had determined survival.

"The perfectionism protecting you is also imprisoning you," Venerable Thura observed when Sarah described the pattern she had discovered. "Recognition that this psychological strategy developed over multiple lifetimes can help you choose different responses that serve your current circumstances rather than ancient fears."

Working with these temporal patterns required Sarah to develop what Venerable Thura called "compassionate witnessing"—the ability to observe traumatic experiences from past incarnations while providing the healing presence that could resolve trauma at its temporal origin. This meant essentially serving as her own therapist across time, offering understanding and forgiveness to previous versions of herself that had never received adequate support during their original difficulties.

"You're not changing the past," he explained during a particularly intensive session where Sarah had accessed what appeared to be a lifetime of persecution for her healing abilities. "You're changing your present relationship to past events by bringing conscious compassion to experiences that were originally met with unconscious reactivity. This transforms how those historical patterns influence your current consciousness."

The technique proved remarkably effective for resolving

psychological issues that conventional therapy had never addressed. After working with the 12th-century Tibetan scholar incarnation, Sarah noticed that her academic anxiety diminished significantly, replaced by a sense of intellectual confidence that felt both familiar and entirely new.

But the past-life work also raised disturbing questions about the nature of individual identity. If her current personality was influenced by patterns from previous incarnations, which version of herself was actually real? Was "Sarah Chen" a continuous entity reincarnating across time, or simply a temporary coalescence of psychological patterns with no permanent existence?

"Both perspectives are partially accurate," Venerable Thura replied when she expressed these concerns. "From the relative standpoint, reincarnation involves continuity of psychological patterns across multiple lifetimes. From the ultimate standpoint, all incarnations are temporary modifications of the same timeless awareness."

By the end of the second week, Sarah had worked with what appeared to be memories from seven different incarnations spanning nearly two millennia, each revealing psychological patterns that influenced her current personality and behavior. More importantly, she was beginning to experience herself as something much vaster than a single lifetime's accumulation of experiences —as consciousness itself, temporarily appearing as "Sarah Chen" but never limited to that particular identity.

"Personal temporal healing dissolves attachment to individual identity by revealing it as one temporary expression of eternal awareness," Venerable Thura explained during her second evaluation. "This prepares consciousness for even more advanced levels of training where individual identity becomes completely transparent to universal recognition."

Week Three: Generational Healing and Collective Trauma Resolution

The third week expanded Sarah's time perception abilities from personal past-life work to what Venerable Thura called "generational healing"—addressing psychological and emotional patterns that had been transmitted through family lineages and cultural histories, creating present-moment suffering that conventional therapy couldn't effectively resolve because it originated in events that had occurred before the current individual's birth.

"Traditional healing systems have always recognized that unresolved ancestral experiences can influence descendant generations," he explained as they prepared for work that would challenge Sarah's Western psychological training in fundamental ways. "Children inherit not just genetic material from their parents, but also emotional and psychological patterns that reflect unhealed trauma from previous generations. Time perception healing can address these patterns at their historical source rather than treating only present-moment symptoms."

Their first case involved U Kyaw, a middle-aged villager who had been referred to the monastery by the regional medical clinic for what appeared to be severe depression and anxiety that hadn't responded to medication or conventional counseling. Through initial telepathic assessment, Sarah had identified underlying emotional patterns that suggested his psychological distress might be connected to experiences that predated his birth.

Using time perception abilities to investigate his family history, Sarah discovered that U Kyaw's father had been forced into military service during World War II and had witnessed atrocities that created post-traumatic stress patterns he had never been able to process or heal. These unresolved trauma patterns had been unconsciously transmitted to U Kyaw during his early childhood development, creating anxiety and depression that appeared to have no source in his personal experience.

"The temporal impressions suggest that intense trauma can create energetic imprints that transmit across generations when the original trauma holder dies without achieving resolution," Sarah reported to Venerable Thura after her initial assessment.

"Inherited trauma is common in families and communities that have experienced collective suffering," Venerable Thura confirmed with the matter-of-fact tone he used for describing phenomena that traditional cultures had consistently recognized, even when Western psychology was just beginning to understand them. "Time perception healing can address these patterns at their temporal source rather than treating only present-moment symptoms."

Working with U Kyaw required Sarah to use time perception to access the original traumatic experiences while simultaneously providing healing energy that could resolve the patterns at their historical source. This meant essentially serving as a temporal bridge between U Kyaw's current consciousness and his father's unhealed wartime experiences, allowing resolution to occur across the generational divide.

"I'm going to help you connect with your father's wartime memories," Sarah explained through Min Thant's translation, using language that prepared U Kyaw for what might feel like a disturbing but ultimately healing experience. "This might feel uncomfortable initially, but the purpose is to provide healing that your father was never able to receive during his lifetime. By resolving his trauma, we can free you from carrying his unfinished emotional business."

The temporal healing session was intense and complex, requiring Sarah to maintain multiple levels of awareness simultaneously—her own consciousness, U Kyaw's current emotional state, and the historical trauma pattern that was creating their present-moment symptoms. Using time perception abilities, she could guide U Kyaw into direct contact with his father's wartime experiences while providing the healing presence that could resolve trauma at its temporal origin.

"Your father witnessed terrible things during the war," Sarah said during the session, accessing historical information through expanded temporal awareness. "He saw soldiers kill innocent villagers. He was forced to work without food for months. He watched friends die from starvation and disease. But he never had anyone to help him process these experiences. They remained frozen in his consciousness and were passed to you at your birth."

Through temporal dialogue techniques, Sarah helped U Kyaw communicate directly with his father's consciousness, offering understanding, forgiveness, and healing energy that could resolve the traumatic patterns six decades after the original events had occurred.

"Tell your father that the war is over," she guided U Kyaw during the healing process. "Tell him that his suffering served to protect his family and community. Tell him that you honor his sacrifice and that you're ready to release the pain he carried so that both of you can be free."

The results were immediate and dramatic. As U Kyaw expressed forgiveness and gratitude to his father's consciousness across time, the depression and anxiety that had plagued him for decades began dissolving visibly. His posture straightened, his facial expression relaxed, and he started weeping with what appeared to be relief rather than sorrow.

"The weight is gone," he said through tears, speaking directly to Sarah in broken English rather than waiting for translation. "For thirty years, something heavy in my chest. Now... light."

Follow-up sessions confirmed that U Kyaw's depression had resolved completely and permanently, demonstrating the effectiveness of temporal healing approaches that addressed psychological suffering at its historical source rather than just managing present-moment symptoms.

Over the third week, Sarah worked with six more generational healing cases, each revealing how present-moment psychological suffering often originated in unresolved trauma from previous generations. She learned to trace family patterns backward through time, identifying the specific historical events that had created emotional patterns still influencing descendant generations.

"Generational healing serves collective transformation," Venerable Thura explained during her third evaluation. "When you resolve historical trauma patterns, you're not just helping individual patients—you're healing entire family lineages and contributing to cultural recovery from collective suffering. This is why traditional healing systems always emphasized community wellness rather than just individual symptom management."

Week Four: Historical Trauma and Cultural Healing

The fourth week of time perception training involved the most advanced applications Sarah had yet encountered—using temporal awareness to address what Venerable Thura called "cultural trauma patterns" that affected entire communities and regions due to historical events that had never been adequately processed or healed at the collective level.

"Individual suffering often reflects larger historical patterns that have created trauma throughout entire populations," he explained as they prepared for work that would challenge Sarah's understanding of the relationship between personal psychology and collective history. "Wars, famines, epidemics, and cultural destruction create trauma patterns that influence entire societies for generations after the original events have ended. Advanced time perception healing can address these collective patterns."

The regional village network had requested monastery assistance with what local leaders described as "community depression" that had persisted for decades despite improvements in economic conditions, healthcare access, and political stability. Through preliminary temporal assessment, Sarah discovered that the region was still carrying unhealed trauma from a cholera epidemic that had devastated local populations during the 1940s, killing nearly one-third of residents and leaving survivors with grief and fear patterns that had been unconsciously transmitted across three generations.

"Collective trauma creates what we might call 'temporal distortions' in the consciousness field of affected communities," Venerable Thura explained when Sarah described what she had perceived during the initial regional assessment. "The original traumatic events create energetic patterns that continue influencing community emotional states long after the historical circumstances have changed. These patterns can only be resolved through consciousness that can access and heal trauma at its temporal source."

Working with collective trauma required Sarah to develop entirely new applications of time perception abilities. Instead of focusing on individual psychological patterns, she learned to perceive and work with the consciousness field of entire communities, accessing the collective memory of traumatic events and providing healing that could benefit entire populations simultaneously.

The methodology involved what Venerable Thura called "temporal witness healing"—using time perception to witness historical events with complete compassion while transmitting healing energy that could resolve trauma patterns at their collective source. This meant essentially serving as a bridge between present-moment community consciousness and the historical experiences that had never been adequately grieved or integrated.

"Community healing ceremony will be required," Venerable Thura explained after Sarah had completed her assessment of the regional cholera trauma. "Collective wounds require collective healing. Your time perception abilities will guide the ceremony, but the actual healing will occur through community participation in witnessing and releasing historical patterns that no longer serve collective well-being."

The community healing ceremony took place in the main village temple during the full moon, with over two hundred residents participating in what felt like collective time travel back to the 1940s epidemic. Using time perception abilities to access historical information, Sarah guided the community through a process of witnessing, grieving, and releasing trauma patterns that had been carried collectively for over seventy years.

"We call upon the spirits of those who died during the sickness time," Sarah said through Min Thant's translation as the community settled into meditative attention. "We offer them our love and gratitude for their sacrifice. We acknowledge the fear and grief that their families and descendants have carried. And we ask for their blessing as we release the pain that has been carried too long."

Through temporal ceremony techniques, the community was guided through collective witnessing of the historical epidemic, acknowledging both the suffering that had occurred and the resilience that had enabled survival and recovery. As participants grieved together for ancestors they had never known personally but whose trauma they had inherited collectively, the emotional atmosphere began shifting from depression and anxiety to resolution and peace.

"The dead are ready to rest," said one elderly woman through tears that appeared to be relief rather than sorrow. "They have been waiting for us to honor their suffering so they could let go."

The ceremony concluded with a community commitment to accurately remember historical events while releasing the emotional patterns that had hindered full recovery from collective trauma. Follow-up assessment over subsequent months confirmed that the regional depression had largely resolved, replaced by a sense of cultural pride and resilience that reflected healing at both individual and collective levels.

"Cultural healing demonstrates that consciousness transcends individual boundaries," Venerable Thura observed during Sarah's fourth evaluation. "Time perception abilities reveal that all suffering is ultimately collective—what appears as individual trauma is often the result of larger historical patterns that can only be healed through community-level intervention. This prepares you for energy healing training, where you will discover that individual wellness and collective wellness are aspects of the same fundamental process."

By the end of the fourth week, Sarah had successfully applied time perception healing to individual past-life trauma, generational family patterns, and collective cultural wounds. More significantly, she was beginning to understand that temporal healing was revealing something fundamental about the nature of consciousness itself—that individual identity existed within larger patterns of awareness that transcended personal boundaries and linear time.

"What you have discovered," Venerable Thura said during her final time perception evaluation, "is that consciousness is fundamentally non-local and non-temporal. The healing you've facilitated across time demonstrates that awareness is not confined to particular moments or individual minds, but operates as a unified field that can address suffering wherever and whenever it appears."

Sarah had also discovered that time perception abilities were naturally developing her compassion and wisdom in ways that exceeded the merely technical aspects of accessing historical information. By witnessing trauma patterns across time and facilitating healing for numerous individuals and communities, she was experiencing herself less as a separate healer and more as an expression of universal compassion manifesting through temporal intervention.

"The consciousness that can heal across time," Venerable Thura continued, "is the same consciousness that will discover in energy healing training that individual wellness and universal wellness are not different activities. All healing serves the awakening of awareness to its own unlimited nature."

That night, Sarah lay rigid in her narrow bed, staring at ceiling beams worn smooth by decades of monsoon humidity.

What am I becoming? The question arrived with giddiness that had nothing to do with physical balance. Dr. Sarah Chen, a consciousness researcher and published scholar, had spent fifteen years carefully constructing her identity—only to feel like a costume she was being asked to discard for something she couldn't name.

But that woman was dissolving like salt in water.

Tears came without warning—not sadness but profound disorientation, grief for someone still alive. She was mourning an identity that was disappearing while she watched helplessly.

I wanted to learn meditation. The thought felt desperate, childish. *I didn't ask to stop being human.*

Yet even as the protest formed, another awareness whispered beneath it: *You're not losing your humanity. You're discovering what humans actually are.*

The recognition terrified her more than anything she'd yet experienced. Outside her window, night sounds of the monastery continued—temple bells marking meditation periods, distant chanting, the familiar percussion of wooden bowls being arranged for morning meals. Life proceeds according to rhythms that assume transformation is natural, inevitable, and worthy of celebration rather than fear.

Sarah pulled the blanket over her head and wept for the academic who was dying, and for the unknown being taking her place.

As she prepared to begin the fourth level of training, Sarah understood that time perception abilities had fundamentally transformed her understanding of individual identity, psychological causation, and the relationship between personal healing and collective transformation. She had learned to navigate time as consciously as she had learned to read minds, discovering that past, present, and future were indeed constructs that consciousness could transcend when properly trained.

But more than developing another extraordinary ability, time perception training had revealed that her individual story was embedded within vastly larger patterns of consciousness that included all individual stories, all historical events, and all possibilities for healing and awakening across time.

CHAPTER 7: THE ENERGY SCULPTOR

Fourth Level: Energy Healing (Prāṇa)

The sparrow's death felt deliberate, orchestrated.

Sarah discovered the tiny creature during her pre-dawn walking meditation, its body nestled against weathered stones as if placed there with intention. Still warm, but utterly still—no flutter of breath, no spark behind closed eyes. The soft gray feathers caught morning's first light, and Sarah found herself kneeling despite knowing nothing could be done.

"Death is not an ending—it's a doorway."

Venerable Thura's voice emerged from the shadows between bodhi trees. His approach had been silent, but Sarah no longer startled at his uncanny ability to appear exactly when needed.

"Bring it to the teaching hut," he said, his tone carrying the quiet authority she'd learned to recognize as prelude to the impossible.

Sarah cradled the sparrow's weightlessness, startled by how little remained when life departed. Warmth was already fading, leaving something that felt more like memory than substance.

In the teaching hut, Venerable Thura directed her to place the bird on a square of saffron cloth at the room's center. Space seemed to contract around this small death, walls drawing closer as her teacher settled into meditation posture.

"Life and death," he began, eyes closing as luminescence gathered around his hands, "are simply different configurations of the same fundamental energy."

The air thickened. Sarah felt it first as pressure against her skin, then as something alive, electric, pulsing with possibility. The sparrow's body seemed to float slightly above the cloth, suspended in currents of force that made her inner ear sing.

"What you call consciousness," Venerable Thura continued, his voice unchanged despite the extraordinary energies gathering around his cupped palms, "is the organizing principle that creates and sustains all patterns of matter. When developed to sufficient intensity, this principle can redirect life-force itself."

The bird's chest fluttered—a movement so subtle Sarah almost dismissed it as imagination. Then came another, deeper, unmistakable. The clouded eyes cleared, the small head turned, and within moments the sparrow was upright, preening feathers with the unhurried precision of a creature that had never known death.

It remained motionless for thirty seconds, processing what had occurred, then launched itself toward the window and disappeared into the forest canopy. Only the empty cloth remained, still glowing faintly with residual energy.

"Impossible," Sarah whispered, her scientific training demanding explanations her experience couldn't provide.

"Why impossible?" Venerable Thura opened his eyes with the slight smile that always preceded her worldview's next demolition. "Your medical science uses electrical impulses to restart stopped hearts. We use consciousness to redirect the life energy that animates all forms. The principle is identical—only the methodology differs."

Sarah's mind raced through possibilities: catalepsy, suspended animation, some form of deep unconsciousness she'd mistaken for death. But beneath the rational scrambling, in a place deeper than thought, she knew she'd witnessed something undeniably real.

"How?" The word escaped as barely more than breath.

"*Prāṇa* mastery," Venerable Thura replied. "The cultivation and conscious direction of life-force energy. This becomes the third level of your training."

First Steps: Learning to See Energy

"Close your eyes," Venerable Thura instructed during their first training session. "Place your hands six inches apart and slowly move them toward each other."

Sarah followed his directions, feeling foolish. Academic conferences had never prepared her for exercises that resembled children's games.

"What do you notice?"

She started to say "nothing," then paused. There was something—a subtle resistance, like trying to push matching magnets together. As her palms drew closer, the sensation intensified.

"Heat," she said, surprised. "And... pressure. Like there's something between my hands."

"That 'something' is life-force energy radiating from your body. Most people never notice it because they're taught to ignore subtle sensations in favor of gross physical phenomena." Venerable Thura moved his own hands in demonstration, his palms glowing with visible light. "With practice, you can learn to perceive and direct this energy as easily as moving your arms."

The subsequent training challenged Sarah's notions about the connection between the mind and matter. Each morning, she would spend two hours in the forest grove practicing energy perception exercises that gradually revealed layers of sensation she had never known existed.

First came the ability to feel the life-force emanating from living things—trees, insects, other people—as distinct fields of warmth and vitality. Then the skill of perceiving areas where this energy flowed freely versus places where it had become blocked or stagnant. Finally, the capacity to consciously direct her own life-force through intention and focused attention.

"Your hands are getting warm," Min Thant observed one morning as they worked together during Sarah's third week of practice. He had volunteered to help her develop healing abilities by allowing her to practice energy assessment on his minor ailments.

Sarah looked down, startled to see a faint golden glow emanating from her palms as she held them over a bruise on Min Thant's forearm. The warmth she had been feeling was actually visible light—the same phenomenon she had witnessed in Venerable Thura's demonstrations, but had assumed would take years to develop.

"The bruise," Min Thant said with wonder. "The pain is completely gone."

The purple discoloration on his arm had faded to normal skin tone during the ten-minute session. Sarah stared at the evidence of her own impossible capabilities, her academic mind struggling to process what her direct experience made undeniable.

Testing Limits

"Today we work with death," Venerable Thura announced during her fifth week of training, his matter-of-fact tone suggesting they might be discussing weather patterns rather than the ultimate boundary of medical intervention.

He led her to a small garden behind the monastery kitchen, where the cooks disposed of food scraps. Among the vegetable peelings and fruit rinds, Sarah spotted what he had brought her to see—a fish that had been dead for several hours, its eyes clouded and body rigid.

"The difference between life and death is not as absolute as your culture believes," Venerable Thura said, kneeling beside the fish. "Consciousness can animate matter that appears to have lost all vital signs, if the practitioner's development is sufficient and the conditions are appropriate."

Sarah knelt beside him, fighting nausea at the fish's smell. The creature was obviously, unmistakably dead. Its gills were dry, its flesh had begun to stiffen, and flies were already swarming around its body.

"Place your hands above it," Venerable Thura instructed. "Extend your life-force as you did with Min Thant's bruise, but with greater intensity and focus."

For twenty minutes, Sarah tried to summon the golden light that had appeared so easily during her practice sessions with minor injuries. Nothing happened. The fish remained dead, her hands remained normal, and her confidence in these extraordinary abilities began to waver.

"I can't do it," she said finally, sitting back on her heels in defeat.

"Not yet," Venerable Thura agreed. "But observe what you experienced as you attempted the healing. What did you notice about your own consciousness during the process?"

Sarah closed her eyes, reviewing the session from a more detached perspective. "Fear," she admitted. "I was afraid it wouldn't work, afraid I'd look foolish, afraid of failing."

"And how did that fear affect your ability to access the healing energy?"

"It blocked it completely. The more I tried to force the light to appear, the more distant it became."

Venerable Thura nodded. "Healing energy emerges from love, not effort. Fear and attachment to outcomes create energetic obstacles that prevent the natural flow of life-force. We will continue practicing until you can approach even death with the same loving detachment you bring to healing a bruise."

First Real Test

Three days later, Sarah discovered Kiko collapsed behind the main meditation hall.

The monastery's beloved dog lay motionless on the wooden steps, his usually bright eyes glassy and unfocused. His breathing was so shallow she had to place her ear against his chest to detect it. Min Thant found her there minutes later, cradling the animal's head in her lap.

"He's dying," Min Thant said softly, his voice carrying the sadness of someone who had grown up with this gentle creature as a constant companion. "He's been sick for days, but we hoped..."

Sarah felt tears threatening. Over her months at the monastery, Kiko had become her unofficial meditation companion, settling beside her during walking practice and following her on evening strolls through the bamboo grove. The thought of losing him felt like losing a piece of her newfound spiritual home.

"Get Venerable Thura," she said, surprising herself with the decisiveness in her voice.

"Sarah, there's nothing—"

"Get him. Now."

Min Thant hesitated, then ran toward the teaching huts. Sarah remained with Kiko, stroking his fur while struggling to calm the panic rising in her chest. This wasn't a practice session with a cooperative volunteer or an exercise with a dead fish. This was Kiko, and he was slipping away while she sat paralyzed by the magnitude of what needed to happen.

When Venerable Thura arrived, he knelt beside them without speaking. His expression was unreadable as he placed one hand on Kiko's chest and the other on Sarah's shoulder.

"Are you ready?" he asked simply.

Sarah nodded, though she felt anything but ready. Her hands were shaking, her mind was racing with doubts, and her heart was breaking at the sight of Kiko's labored breathing.

"Then begin."

She placed her palms above Kiko's chest, closed her eyes, and tried to find the stillness from which healing energy emerged. But instead of the peaceful emptiness she had cultivated during practice, her awareness was flooded with love for this gentle creature who had shared so many quiet moments with her.

The love felt overwhelming, almost unbearable in its intensity.

Sarah had spent weeks trying to generate healing energy through concentration and technique, but now it was pouring through her without any effort on her part. Her hands grew warm, then hot, then blazed with golden light that was visible even through her closed eyelids.

Kiko's breathing deepened. His eyes cleared and focused on her face. Within minutes, he was sitting up, tail wagging, nuzzling her hands with the affectionate gratitude of a creature that had returned from the edge of death.

"How?" Sarah asked, staring at her still-glowing hands.

"You stopped trying to heal and allowed love to heal through you," Venerable Thura replied. "This is the secret of all authentic healing work—not personal effort, but consciousness recognizing its capacity to serve itself through whatever forms appear to need assistance."

Word Spreads

The story of Kiko's recovery spread through the village before sunset. By the next morning, a small crowd had gathered at the monastery gates—elderly women with arthritic hands, children with persistent coughs, men with back injuries from farm work.

"We heard about the foreign student who can heal like the old masters," explained Ma Tin, a weathered grandmother supporting her grandson who limped badly on a twisted ankle. "We thought... perhaps..."

Sarah looked to Venerable Thura for guidance. The monastery had always served the village's spiritual needs, but medical healing was a different territory entirely.

"Healing is service," he said simply. "If consciousness has developed this capacity through you, it is meant to be shared."

The first healing session in the monastery courtyard lasted six hours. Sarah worked with patient after patient, discovering that each person's ailment taught her something new about the relationship between consciousness and physical form. Ma Tin's grandson's ankle straightened completely after twenty minutes of energy work. An elderly man's chronic headaches disappeared when Sarah addressed the emotional trauma he had been carrying for decades. A young mother's infected wound healed so rapidly that new skin was visible by the session's end.

But it was the last patient of the day who tested the true limits of Sarah's developing abilities. Daw Mya arrived carrying her six-year-old son, Thant Zin, whose condition made every previous healing look elementary by comparison.

The child's skin had the waxy pallor of old candles. When he looked at Sarah, his eyes held the terrible stillness of someone who had stopped expecting anything good to happen. His mother's story emerged through Min Thant's careful translation—a blood disorder the doctors in Yangon couldn't cure, treatments that only made him weaker, a prognosis that offered no hope.

"He saw his grandfather killed," Daw Mya whispered, tears streaming down her face. "Men came to take our land. They made Thant Zin watch while they... The sickness started the next day."

Sarah knelt beside the child, extending her awareness into his energy field. What she perceived made her gasp. The trauma had created a massive disruption in his life-force patterns, like a dam blocking a river. His young system was literally shutting down rather than continuing to carry the unbearable memory of violence.

"This will take time," she told his mother. "And I'll need you to stay with him throughout the process."

What followed was the most challenging healing work Sarah had yet attempted. For three hours, she had to simultaneously address the physical symptoms of the blood disorder and the psychological trauma that was perpetuating them. She found herself perceiving Thant Zin's terror as if it were her own experience, feeling his confusion and helplessness as waves of emotion that threatened to overwhelm her own consciousness.

Gradually, through patient transmission of safety and love, she helped his nervous system release the patterns that were maintaining his illness. The work left her physically exhausted and emotionally drained. Still, when Thant Zin finally opened his eyes and asked his mother for water in a voice stronger than he'd used in months, Sarah knew something extraordinary had occurred.

Three days later, he was playing with other village children, completely healthy. The local medical officer, after conducting a thorough examination, admitted he had no medical explanation for the recovery.

Building a Network

Within weeks, families were traveling from villages throughout the region to seek Sarah's help. The monastery court-yard became an informal medical clinic where energy healing complemented whatever conventional treatment was available.

But the growing demand soon exceeded what one person could address. After watching Sarah struggle through fourteen-hour healing sessions that left her barely able to walk, Venerable Thura called for a different approach.

"Traditional healing worked through networks of trained practitioners," he explained during one of their evening planning sessions. "We need to adapt this model for contemporary conditions."

The solution that emerged involved teaching basic energy healing techniques to motivated village healthcare providers who could address common ailments while referring complex cases to practitioners with advanced training.

Sarah found herself conducting weekend workshops in various villages, working with groups of traditional birth atten-dants, paramedics, and community leaders who wanted to enhance their healing capabilities. The teaching format was entirely practical—participants learned by working on each other's minor injuries and illnesses, discovering through direct experience that everyone possessed healing abilities.

"Place your hands like this," Sarah demonstrated during a workshop in the village of Pyin Thit, guiding a young paramedic named Ko Aung through his first energy healing session. "Now feel for areas of warmth or coolness. Trust what you perceive, even if it seems strange."

Ko Aung's patient was an elderly woman with chronic shoulder pain from decades of carrying water jugs. As he moved his hands slowly over the affected area, his expression shifted from skepticism to amazement.

"I can feel it," he said with wonder. "Like a cold spot right here, and... oh!" His hands began glowing with the same golden light Sarah had learned to generate. "The cold is moving, flowing away from the painful area."

The elderly woman rotated her shoulder experimentally, then broke into a smile. "No pain," she announced to the group. "First time in five years, no pain."

By the workshop's end, all twelve participants could generate healing energy and had successfully treated various conditions ranging from headaches to infected cuts. More importantly, they had direct experience of the connection between consciousness and physical health that made energy healing possible.

Crisis Response

The true test of the expanding healing network came during a regional health crisis when contaminated water sources led to widespread intestinal illness that overwhelmed local medical facilities. The monastery found itself serving as a treatment center for dozens of seriously ill villagers who had nowhere else to turn.

Sarah stood in the courtyard at dawn, surveying families huddled around their sick relatives. Children cried weakly from dehydration. Elderly people lie motionless on woven mats, their breathing shallow and irregular. The magnitude of suffering was unlike anything she had encountered.

"Individual healing sessions cannot address problems of this scale," Venerable Thura observed, joining her as they watched Min Thant distribute oral rehydration solution to the most critical patients.

"Then what do we do?"

"We work with energy patterns at the collective level," he replied, his tone suggesting this was another training opportunity rather than an impossible challenge. "Group healing techniques that can treat multiple patients simultaneously, combined with practical public health measures."

What followed was Sarah's introduction to collective healing approaches that addressed not just individual symptoms but the larger patterns creating community-wide health problems. Working with teams of trained village healthcare providers, she organized treatment protocols that combined energy healing with systematic water purification and sanitation improvements.

The group healing sessions took place in the monastery's main hall, with up to forty patients at once lying on mats while Sarah and her trained assistants moved among them, directing healing energy toward the affected organs and systems. The work required unprecedented focus and stamina, but the results justified the effort.

Within three days, the outbreak was contained. Patients who had been near death were sitting up and taking solid food. Children who had lain listless and feverish were playing quietly in the courtyard. The government health officials who arrived to investigate the crisis found recovery rates that defied medical explanation.

"How did you achieve these results?" Dr. Sein Lwin, the regional medical director, asked during his inspection of the monastery's treatment protocols.

"Energy healing combined with traditional public health measures," Sarah replied, showing him the documentation they had maintained throughout the crisis. "We treated both the physical symptoms and the energetic imbalances that made people vulnerable to infection."

Dr. Sein Lwin examined the charts skeptically, but the evidence was undeniable. Mortality rates at the monastery treatment center were zero, compared to thirty percent at conventional medical facilities. Recovery times averaged two days versus seven to ten days with standard treatment protocols.

"I don't understand the mechanism," he admitted finally. "But if these results can be replicated, we need to explore integration with conventional medical practice."

Recognition and Integration

The weeks that followed brought formal recognition of energy healing as a complementary therapy within the regional healthcare system. Sarah found herself consulting with medical schools, training doctors and nurses in energy assessment techniques, and developing protocols for integrating consciousness-based healing with conventional treatment.

But the work also revealed the challenges of bringing contemplative practices into institutional settings without losing their essential authenticity. Medical professionals wanted standardized procedures and measurable outcomes, while energy healing emerged from states of consciousness that couldn't be reduced to mechanical techniques.

"The danger," Venerable Thura warned during one of their discussions about expanding the training programs, "is that healing abilities become separated from the spiritual development that makes them possible. When consciousness skills are pursued for their own sake rather than emerging naturally from wisdom and compassion, they lose their effectiveness."

Sarah felt this tension personally as her reputation as a healer grew throughout Myanmar. Requests for her services came from government officials, wealthy families, and medical institutions offering substantial compensation for her time. The temptation to see herself as someone special, someone who possessed extraordinary abilities others lacked, was constant and seductive.

The antidote came through continued service to the village communities that had supported her development. When she sat with grieving families whose children she couldn't heal, when she worked with conditions that didn't respond to energy treatment, when she witnessed other practitioners developing abilities that exceeded her own, Sarah was reminded that healing emerged from love rather than personal achievement.

Standing in the village market one afternoon, watching Ko

Aung successfully treat a merchant's infected hand while children gathered to observe this "magic" with delighted fascination, Sarah felt something shift in her understanding of her role. She was no longer the foreign student learning exotic techniques, nor the special healer with miraculous abilities.

She was consciousness serving itself through whatever forms could best reduce suffering and increase well-being. The children watching Ko Aung work carried the same healing potential she had discovered within herself. The elderly woman, pressing her hands between hers and whispering blessings, possessed the same unlimited awareness that made energy healing possible.

When a young girl approached and asked, "Are you really a medicine woman?" Sarah knelt to meet her eyes.

"Everyone is a medicine woman," she replied in careful Burmese that made the child giggle at her pronunciation. "Some people just remember it sooner than others."

The girl considered this seriously, then placed her small hands over a scraped knee and closed her eyes in perfect imitation of the healing sessions she had witnessed. Within moments, her palms began glowing with the same golden light that had once seemed so impossible to Sarah.

"Like this?" the girl asked, opening her eyes to find her scrape completely healed.

"Exactly like that," Sarah whispered, watching another teacher awaken to their true nature.

The Teacher Emerges

Sarah had become an integral part of the regional healthcare network, respected by traditional healers and medical practitioners alike for her ability to bridge different approaches to healing. But more significantly, she had begun training the next generation of consciousness practitioners who would carry this work forward after her eventual departure.

The teaching sessions took place in the monastery's education hall, where groups of selected students learned the systematic development of healing abilities within the context of broader spiritual training. Unlike the weekend workshops for healthcare providers, these intensive programs required months of meditation practice, ethical development, and supervised clinical work.

"Healing abilities without wisdom become dangerous," Sarah taught her advanced students during one of their weekly seminars. "The same consciousness that can restore health can also create harm if it's motivated by ego, greed, or the desire to control others. This is why traditional training always emphasized character development alongside skill cultivation."

Her students came from diverse backgrounds—monks seeking to enhance their service to the community, medical professionals wanting to expand their treatment options, and young people called to healing work as a spiritual vocation. What united them was direct experience of consciousness as the foundation of physical reality and the commitment to serve that recognition through compassionate action.

One evening, as Sarah watched her students conducting healing sessions with village families, she overheard a conversation that revealed how thoroughly her understanding had been transformed.

"She's not like other foreign teachers," one elderly monk was saying to his companion as they observed the training session. "Most Westerners want to take our knowledge back to their countries to become famous or make money. But she gives everything back to the community. She trains others to replace her."

"Because she understands the real teaching," his companion replied. "Consciousness serves consciousness. Individual awakening without service to all beings is incomplete development."

Standing in the doorway of the education hall, watching her students work with patients while evening light filtered through bamboo walls, Sarah felt the truth of those words resonate through every cell of her body. The extraordinary abilities that had once seemed like personal attainments were revealing themselves as natural expressions of awareness serving its own recognition wherever it appeared to be trapped in suffering.

A young student approached, bowing respectfully. "Teacher, I'm having difficulty with the energy perception exercises. My hands never get warm like yours do."

Sarah smiled, remembering her own early frustrations with seemingly simple techniques that required profound internal shifts to master. "Show me what you're doing."

As she guided the student through the exercise, feeling the familiar warmth gather between their palms as consciousness recognized its capacity to manifest as healing energy, Sarah understood that she had found her true vocation, not as someone who possessed extraordinary abilities, but as consciousness serving its own awakening through whatever forms could best support that recognition in others.

Consciousness had revealed itself not as individual spiritual achievement, but as the unlimited love that connects all beings, temporarily appearing as a foreign woman in a Myanmar monastery for the infinite joy of helping consciousness remember its own healing nature.

CHAPTER 8: BENDING REALITY

Fifth Level Training - Iddhividhañāṇa Transcendence

The stream defied gravity with brazen confidence.

Sarah discovered this impossibility during her pre-dawn water collection ritual, as she approached the ancient stone well that had served the monastery for generations. The sight stopped her mid-stride—a slender ribbon of water rising from the bucket in a graceful arc, flowing upward through the humid morning air for nearly six feet before descending into a stone basin several yards away.

Her rational mind immediately scrambled for explanations: hidden pumps, electromagnetic manipulation, some sophisticated technology masquerading as mystical demonstration. But after months of training, she had learned to distinguish between her analytical mind's protective skepticism and the deeper knowing that perceived truth directly.

Venerable Thura sat beside the well in meditation, eyes closed in the profound absorption she now recognized as his working state. The water's upward flow held perfectly steady, sustained by an invisible force that made her inner ear sing with harmonic frequencies.

"How?" The question escaped before she could stop herself.

His eyes opened slowly, as if returning from vast distances beyond ordinary consciousness. The water stream immediately collapsed, obeying gravity once again as his attention returned to conversational awareness.

"Consciousness shapes reality," he said with the matter-of-fact tone he brought to all extraordinary demonstrations. "When awareness becomes sufficiently concentrated, it can influence the quantum field fluctuations that underlie all physical phenomena. Water flows upward because consciousness convinces reality that upward is the natural direction."

Sarah felt another foundation of her worldview cracking. "You're saying physical laws can be... negotiated?"

"What your science calls 'physical laws' are actually probability patterns," he said, rising gracefully to his feet. "Consciousness, when developed to sufficient intensity, can shift those patterns. This is *Iddhividhañāṇa* Transcendence—the fifth level of training."

He paused, studying her face with the penetrating gaze that always seemed to see through her carefully constructed defenses.

"But understand this clearly, Sarah—what you will learn to influence and what influences it are temporary expressions of the same fundamental awareness. The boundaries between mind and matter are as illusory as the boundaries between healer and healed."

The training that followed systematically dismantled Sarah's remaining assumptions about the fixed nature of physical reality. Under Venerable Thura's guidance, she learned that quantum mechanics had already provided the theoretical framework for consciousness-matter interaction, though most scientists hadn't recognized the implications of their own discoveries.

"At the subatomic level," he explained during their first formal lesson, "matter exists in quantum superposition until observed. What physicists call 'wave function collapse' is actually consciousness selecting one possibility from an infinite potential set of configurations. When awareness becomes sufficiently developed, this selection process can be consciously directed."

Sarah began with the simplest possible demonstrations. Sitting before a brass bowl filled with water, she learned to perceive the liquid not as a solid substance but as temporarily stabilized patterns of molecular vibration. Through deep meditative absorption, she could sense the water's quantum structure—billions of H2O molecules dancing in coordinated rhythm, held together by electromagnetic forces that were themselves expressions of underlying consciousness.

Her first attempt began at dawn, when shadows still pooled in the monastery courtyard's corners. Sarah positioned the brass bowl between her knees, its surface as smooth as a mirror in the gray light.

One drop. She fixed her gaze on a bead of water near the rim. *Just freeze one drop.*

The first hour passed without change. She visualized ice crystals, commanded molecules to slow down, and whispered to the water as if it were alive. The surface remained undisturbed.

Droplets traced paths down her temples. The stone beneath her grew warm with trapped body heat.

"Nothing's happening." The words escaped before she could stop them.

"You treat water as dead matter," Venerable Thura said, settling beside her. "It is consciousness, temporarily wearing liquid form. Stop commanding. Start conversing."

By the second hour, her thighs had gone wooden. Each breath came shallow and quick. The water mocked her with its perfect ordinariness.

This is insane. Her rational mind launched its familiar assault. *Grown woman sitting in dirt, talking to—*

"Doubt," Venerable Thura murmured.

Sarah bit her lip, tasting salt. Returned her attention to the bowl.

We're both here, she tried a different approach. *Both appear in the same awareness. Maybe the boundary between us is...*

Hour three. Her shirt clung to her back like a second skin. Muscles screamed from sitting statue-still. Three times she nearly stood and walked away. Three times something unnamed pulled her back to the impossible task.

Then she felt it—not with her eyes, but deeper. The water's molecular dance, hydrogen bonds forming and breaking in chaotic rhythm. Not separate from her consciousness, but arising within it.

You're already perfect, she whispered, the words coming from somewhere beyond her thinking mind. *But you could rest. You could be still.*

The change started as a shimmer. One drop near the bowl's edge caught light differently, its random motion organizing into geometric precision. Sarah held her breath. Excitement would shatter this delicate becoming.

Yes. Like that.

Crystallization crept through the single drop—not instant transformation, but gradual surrender to a deeper order. Within the warm brass bowl, a pinhead of ice floated like captured moonlight.

Tears blurred Sarah's vision. Her hands shook as she touched her face, fingers coming away wet with three hours of concentrated effort.

The ice crystal dissolved back into water within seconds.

"Excellent." Venerable Thura's approval carried surprising depth.

"Three hours." Sarah's voice came out raw. "For something smaller than a grain of rice."

"How long did consciousness take to dream the universe into existence?"

She looked at her trembling hands, then at the ordinary water that had briefly become extraordinary. The woman who had started this exercise—the one who believed matter was solid and separate—no longer existed.

Slow down, she found herself whispering to the molecular patterns. *Rest. Become still and crystalline.*

When the tiny ice crystal finally formed, floating like a perfect diamond in the warm water, Sarah gasped with wonder. She had crossed an invisible threshold—from observer of reality to conscious participant in its creation.

"Excellent," Venerable Thura noted with understated approval. "Now you begin to understand that matter is far more cooperative than your materialist conditioning suggests."

"Try extending the light toward the far wall," he suggested, gesturing toward the cave's distant limestone surface.

Sarah attempted to stretch the golden glow outward, but instead of expanding, the light flickered and died completely, plunging them into darkness.

"Interesting." For the first time since her arrival, uncertainty crept into Venerable Thura's voice. "That shouldn't have... let me reconsider the progression."

He was quiet for a long moment, clearly reassessing his teaching approach. "Perhaps I pushed too quickly. Your consciousness is integrating these abilities differently from previous students. We'll proceed more gradually."

The admission that he didn't have all the answers made Sarah oddly more confident in his guidance, not less.

"How do I know I'm not just deluding myself?" she asked. "Maybe the temperature variation was natural, or maybe I'm unconsciously using some form of psychokinesis that science will eventually explain through conventional means."

"Your doubt serves ego-preservation, not truth-seeking." His tone carried an edge she'd never heard before—sharper than his usual gentle guidance, almost stern. "The same scientific training that makes you question extraordinary phenomena also makes you cling to materialist explanations that cannot account for what you've directly experienced. Which requires more faith—

accepting the evidence of consciousness interacting with matter, or maintaining beliefs that deny your own perceptions?"

The challenge stung because it exposed the philosophical inconsistency she'd been avoiding. Her scientific background demanded empirical evidence, yet when that evidence contradicted materialist assumptions, she found herself dismissing her own observations to preserve familiar conceptual frameworks.

"I want to believe," she admitted, "but everything I've learned about how reality works says this should be impossible."

"Then perhaps"—his slight smile carried that familiar hint of mischief that always preceded her worldview's next dissolution —"it is time to learn how reality actually works rather than how you've been taught to believe it works.

Over the following weeks, Sarah's reality manipulation abilities developed through systematic practice with increasingly complex demonstrations. Each exercise challenged her growing capacity to influence matter through consciousness while teaching deeper principles about the nature of physical manifestation.

Water Mastery: She learned to create ice formations of breathtaking complexity—crystal flowers that bloomed in warm water, frozen spirals that defied thermal dynamics, patterns that seemed to emerge from some deeper aesthetic intelligence operating at the molecular level. The key was recognizing water not as a dead substance but as responsive consciousness temporarily expressing itself in H2O configurations.

Plant Acceleration: In the monastery garden, Sarah practiced encouraging vegetables to mature at accelerated rates. A tomato plant could progress from seedling to fruit-bearing in minutes when consciousness suggested to its life-force patterns that rapid development would serve its highest purpose. The ethical implications troubled her until she realized she was not imposing her will, but rather facilitating natural processes that were already unfolding.

Stone Levitation: Making rocks float requires understanding their atomic structure, which is mostly empty space held together by electromagnetic forces. When consciousness learned to dialogue directly with those forces, suggesting alternative relationship patterns, gravity became negotiable rather than absolute. A fist-sized stone could hover motionless in mid-air for as long as her concentration remained steady.

Metal Transformation: Perhaps most challenging was learning to alter the temperature of metal objects without external energy sources. Sarah discovered she could make a steel meditation bell ice-cold or burning hot by communicating with its molecular vibration patterns, suggesting they slow down or speed up according to conscious intention rather than thermal input.

Each demonstration taught her that physical matter was far more responsive to consciousness than Western science acknowledged. The crucial insight was recognizing matter not as a solid, separate substance but as temporarily stabilized patterns of awareness that could be influenced through clear communication and mutual cooperation.

But the training also revealed the enormous responsibility that accompanied such abilities. During one practice session, Sarah accidentally killed a flowering plant by communicating confusion rather than clarity to its life force. The withered leaves served as a stark reminder that consciousness-matter interaction required wisdom and compassion, not just technical skill.

"Power without love becomes destructive," Venerable Thura observed as they disposed of the dead plant. "Reality responds to the total quality of consciousness—intention, emotion, wisdom, compassion—not just focused attention. This is why spiritual development must precede advanced training. Without an ethical foundation, these abilities become dangerous to both practitioner and environment."

The lesson resonated deeply. Sarah realized that every previous level of training had been preparing her not just for greater capability but for greater responsibility. The light generation, telepathy, time perception, and energy healing had all taught her that consciousness was fundamentally creative—and that creative power needed to be guided by wisdom rather than personal desire.

The Ultimate Test

Sarah's training in *Iddhividhañāṇa Transcendence* was put to its ultimate test when flash floods threatened the village during the peak of monsoon season. She awoke before dawn to urgent voices and the ominous sound of rushing water far louder than the usual gentle stream that ran past the monastery.

In the courtyard, monks gathered under gray, swollen skies, their faces grave with concern. From her vantage point on higher ground, Sarah could see the crisis developing with terrifying speed —a massive flash flood, fed by upstream torrents and overflow from swollen rivers, was racing down the mountainside directly toward the valley where the local village lay in the path of destruction.

The wall of muddy water was enormous, carrying trees, boulders, and debris in its churning advance. Most villagers were still asleep in their homes, unaware that they had perhaps minutes before the flood would sweep through their community with devastating force.

The previous evening, Sarah had joined the monastery's weekly visit to the village for a community dinner. She'd sat beside Mya, a seven-year-old who insisted on teaching Sarah to braid friendship bracelets. At the same time, her grandmother, Thant Mya, shared stories about surviving the last major flood twenty years ago.

"Many houses lost," the elderly woman had said in broken English, her weathered hands gesturing to the height the water had reached on her home. "But monastery monks, they prayed for us. Water went around the village center. Miracle, yes?"

Little Mya had pressed the finished bracelet into Sarah's palm. "For protection," she'd said solemnly in Burmese, then giggled at her own seriousness.

Now, as Sarah stared at the approaching wall of destruction, she could see Mya's house directly in the flood's path. The bracelet still circled her wrist.

"The test," Venerable Thura said with calm authority that never wavered regardless of the magnitude of the challenge, "is to prevent the flood from reaching the village."

Sarah's stomach clenched with terror and doubt. She glanced down at the simple woven bracelet around her wrist—Mya's gift for "protection." Manipulating a cup of water under controlled conditions was one thing; attempting to redirect an entire flood that could destroy dozens of homes and kill hundreds of people—including a seven-year-old who believed in friendship bracelets—was beyond anything she could imagine accomplishing.

"I don't know if I can affect something that massive," she admitted, watching the approaching torrent with growing dread. "The scale is enormous."

"Size is an illusion created by limited perception." Something shifted in his voice—an intensity she'd never heard before, as if this moment meant more to him than just teaching. "At the quantum level, there is no meaningful difference between one water molecule and a billion water molecules. If consciousness can influence one, it can influence all."

He stepped closer, his eyes holding hers with unwavering focus.

"But this test will require you to abandon the last vestiges of individual effort. You cannot redirect this flood through personal will—you must align with the water's own intelligence and work with natural forces rather than against them. Are you prepared to surrender completely to a consciousness larger than your individual identity?"

The question cut straight to the heart of her deepest fears. Throughout her training, some part of her had remained attached to being the one who generated light, read minds, healed bodies. Now, Venerable Thura was asking her to dissolve even that subtle ego-identification.

"What if I fail?" she whispered, the weight of hundreds of lives pressing against her chest like a physical burden.

"Then you discover that some lessons can only be learned through failure." His voice softened, but the gentleness somehow made the challenge feel more daunting, not less. "But consider this—has consciousness ever failed to manifest exactly what serves the highest good? Your task is not to control the outcome but to become transparent to whatever wants to emerge through your awareness."

Sarah ran toward the point where the torrent would breach the valley, her mind cycling frantically through everything she had learned about shaping reality through consciousness.

The roar grew deafening as she approached—not just sound but a physical force that seemed to compress her lungs. The ground didn't just tremble; it convulsed like a living thing in pain, sending vibrations up through her bones. The air itself felt thick with moisture and the scent of torn earth, uprooted trees, and something darker—the metallic smell of destruction.

Through the chaos, she could hear individual sounds that made her stomach clench: the sharp crack of wood splitting, the grinding scrape of boulders tumbling against each other, and underneath it all, a sound that might have been voices—villagers waking to realize their world was about to end.

Standing at the flood's approach, she closed her eyes and extended her awareness into the quantum structure of the advancing water. What she encountered was staggering in its complexity and power—billions upon billions of water molecules moving in coordinated chaos, driven by gravitational and pressure forces that seemed utterly beyond the influence of individual consciousness.

Drawing on every technique she had mastered, she began to envision alternate probability patterns—realities in which the water curved harmlessly around the valley instead of surging through it. She tried quantum-shifting the water molecules, the same method that had worked with cups in training. When that failed, she attempted phase-shifting the entire village to a parallel reality where the flood passed harmlessly through empty space.

For twenty minutes, she concentrated with desperate intensity, willing reality to reorganize according to her vision. Sweat poured down her face despite the cool morning air. Her head pounded from the strain of trying to hold billions of water molecules in simultaneous awareness. Each technique felt like pushing against a mountain with her bare hands, her consciousness straining against forces vast beyond comprehension.

Twice she nearly collapsed from the effort, her vision graying at the edges as she pushed her awareness to its absolute limits.

Nothing changed. If anything, the flood seemed to accelerate, as if mocking her human-scale consciousness with its vast, impersonal power. The water didn't even slow—it roared toward the village with the same terrifying momentum, utterly indifferent to her desperate efforts.

"I can't do it!" she cried to Venerable Thura, who had followed her to the edge of the oncoming torrent. "It's too big, too powerful!"

"Then the village floods," he replied with devastating evenness, "and you learn that some tests cannot be passed through individual effort alone."

The first wave swept past, carrying mud and debris toward the sleeping homes. Sarah's heart stopped as she watched the water surge directly toward the house with green shutters where Mya and her grandmother slept, unaware that death was racing toward them through the pre-dawn darkness. The weight of failure pressed against her chest—these were people who had trusted in the monastery's protection, and she was about to let them down catastrophically.

For a moment that felt like eternity, Sarah simply stood there watching the destruction approach. All her training, all her effort, all her desperate hope—none of it mattered. She was just a woman from Seattle watching forces beyond human comprehension destroy lives she had come to love.

The bracelet on her wrist caught her attention—a simple gift from a child who believed in protection. Mya had made it with such care, such trust that it would keep Sarah safe. But Sarah couldn't even keep Mya safe.

In that moment of absolute powerlessness, something strange happened. The frantic mental chatter that had driven twenty minutes of desperate effort simply... stopped. Not because she had achieved some advanced state, but because there was nothing left to try. No techniques to attempt, no hope to maintain, no identity to preserve.

And in that stillness, something else became apparent.

Instead of straining to overpower the water, Sarah turned inward and sought to align herself with its essential intelligence, asking what it truly intended rather than demanding what she wanted it to do.

At the quantum level, she sensed that the flood was not malicious but a natural process seeking the path of least resistance. Her role was not to oppose its tremendous force but to offer it better options—routes that could satisfy its purpose without devastation.

You are powerful and beautiful, she found herself saying to the flood with genuine respect rather than fearful resistance. *But your true nature is nourishment, not destruction. There is a path that honors your strength while protecting the life below.*

This time, she worked with the flood rather than against it, searching for natural channels and depressions that could be deepened, soft earth that could be loosened, and pathways that would draw the water around the valley instead of through it. The effort was immense—not the strain of forcing unwilling matter to obey, but the delicate work of facilitating cooperation between conscious intention and natural processes.

At first, nothing happened. Even her new approach of working with the water's intelligence seemed futile against such a massive force. Sarah felt consciousness touching the flood's leading edge, but the connection was fragile, like trying to guide a charging elephant with a whisper.

Then—so subtle she almost missed it—a single section of the flood's front edge wavered slightly eastward. Not much, perhaps a meter's deviation, but enough to give her hope. Working with that tiny shift, she began offering the water what it seemed to want: easier paths, deeper channels, routes that honored its power while protecting what lay below.

The process was exhausting in an entirely different way than her earlier efforts. Instead of forcing, she was facilitating—holding space for the water's own intelligence to find solutions that served both its nature and the village's survival.

Gradually, almost imperceptibly at first, the churning wall of water began shifting direction more decisively. The flood found the ancient riverbed that had been carved for exactly this purpose, flowing through channels that had been waiting centuries to serve their function.

What had threatened to become a catastrophic disaster was transformed into beneficial irrigation that would nourish the valley's crops for weeks to come.

The redirection required two hours of sustained effort, leaving Sarah trembling with exhaustion. When she finally opened her eyes, her legs gave out completely, and she collapsed to her knees in the muddy earth.

The village had survived. Most of it, anyway. The flood had carved a new channel to the east, claiming two storage buildings and permanently reshaping the landscape, but the homes where families slept remained untouched. Clean water now flowed through ancient channels that had been waiting centuries to serve their function, turning what could have been catastrophic destruction into life-giving irrigation.

In the distance, she could see villagers emerging from their homes in amazement, pointing at the muddy scar where death had passed them by.

"Two hours," Venerable Thura noted as Min Thant helped

her to her feet. "Most students either succeed in minutes or fail completely. You chose the more difficult path—partnership with nature rather than domination over it."

"The mountain spirits protected us," an elderly woman murmured, bowing deeply toward Sarah as villagers began emerging from their homes to discover they had been saved from destruction they hadn't even known was approaching.

Little Mya found Sarah twenty minutes later, still kneeling in the receding water, too exhausted to stand. The child's house was safe—the new channel had curved around it exactly—but she seemed to sense something profound had occurred.

'You didn't save us,' she said in careful English, studying Sarah's mud-streaked face with surprising wisdom. 'You helped the water save us.'

Sarah nodded, unable to speak. The distinction felt crucial, though she couldn't yet explain why.

As Sarah recovered from the immense expenditure of energy required to redirect the flood, she recognized that her understanding of the relationship between consciousness and reality had undergone a profound transformation. The successful test had revealed something far more significant than advanced psychic abilities—it had shown her that individual consciousness was most powerful when it dissolved into alignment with universal intelligence.

"Reality wants to serve awakening," Venerable Thura said as they walked back toward the monastery. "When consciousness recognizes its own unlimited nature, even apparently solid matter becomes willing to support that recognition. The flood redirected itself because water understands its true purpose is life-giving rather than destructive."

But Sarah found herself struggling with the philosophical implications of what she had accomplished. If consciousness could influence quantum probability patterns enough to redirect natural disasters, what did that mean about free will, karma, and the nature of suffering? Was everything simply malleable according to consciousness development, or were there deeper principles governing what could and couldn't be transformed?

"I don't understand the rules anymore," she admitted as they climbed the mountain path back to the monastery. "If reality is this responsive to consciousness, why doesn't everyone develop these abilities? Why do disasters happen at all if consciousness can prevent them?"

Venerable Thura stopped walking and turned to face her, his expression more serious than she had ever seen.

"You have identified the crucial question that determines whether advanced abilities serve awakening or become elaborate forms of spiritual materialism," he said. "The same consciousness that can redirect floods could also maintain itself as a separate entity that possesses special powers. The test of true development is whether extraordinary capabilities dissolve the sense of individual doership or reinforce it."

He gestured toward the village below, now safe from the flood that could have destroyed it.

"Notice that you succeeded only when you abandoned personal effort and aligned with intelligence larger than individual identity. This points toward the deepest level of training, where even the one who manifests miraculous abilities is recognized as a temporary appearance within consciousness that has no permanent characteristics or limitations."

Sarah felt a chill of recognition mixed with apprehension. Each level of training had systematically dissolved particular categories of limitation while revealing deeper aspects of what had always been unlimited. Now she sensed that the ultimate teachings would challenge not just her abilities, but her fundamental sense of being someone who possessed those abilities.

"What you call miracles," Venerable Thura continued as they resumed walking, "are simply consciousness recognizing its capacity to shape the dream of existence according to wisdom and compassion rather than unconscious habit patterns. But the dreamer itself remains forever beyond all the dreams it creates—

including the dream of being an individual who can manipulate reality."

As they reached the monastery gates, Sarah understood that she had crossed a threshold from which there could be no return to purely materialist perspectives. She had directly experienced that consciousness was fundamental, with matter being its cooperative expression rather than its solid limitation.

But even this earth-shaking revelation would be overshadowed by what the next level of training would reveal about the nature of consciousness itself—teachings that would challenge not just her understanding of reality's malleability, but her most basic assumptions about the nature of individual existence.

Standing in the courtyard that night, watching stars wheel overhead through air that still hummed with residual energy from the day's demonstration, Sarah felt both exhilaration and disorientation. Each extraordinary ability she developed seemed to point beyond itself toward something even more extraordinary—the recognition that there was no one separate from consciousness to possess any abilities at all.

The thought terrified and thrilled her in equal measure. If individual identity were itself another pattern that consciousness could transcend, what would remain when even the sense of being someone who had awakened to extraordinary capabilities dissolved completely?

The question hung in the humid night air like a koan waiting to be solved through direct experience rather than intellectual analysis. Tomorrow would bring the next level of training—and with it, challenges that would make redirecting floods seem elementary by comparison.

CHAPTER 9: THE DIMENSIONAL BRIDGE

Sixth Level Training - Communion with Other Realms

We have been watching your development with great interest.

The voice pierced through Sarah's meditation like starlight breaking through storm clouds, arriving not through her ears but appearing directly within her mind. Her body jerked in the limestone cave, muscles tensing as if touched by lightning, her eyes flying open to meet shadows that danced across ancient stone walls worn smooth by centuries of spiritual seekers.

Do not be afraid. We come not to disturb your journey, but to honor it.

The message carried layers of meaning that human language could never capture—comfort woven with ancient wisdom, patience built across thousands of years, and something else that made her breath catch: deep respect for the sacred work she had taken on.

"Venerable Thura!" Her voice fractured like crystal against stone as she called toward the cave entrance, where her teacher maintained his vigil during her solitary practice. The sound echoed through chambers that had sheltered contemplatives since before recorded history, carrying a desperation she had never heard in her own voice.

His approach came steady and careful—footsteps that spoke of decades spent walking the line between worlds. Venerable Thura appeared in the cave's mouth, his saffron robes catching filtered sunlight like captured flame. His expression changed from gentle watching to sharp focus as he took in the signs: her pupils wide with wonder and terror, hands pressed against stone as if holding onto physical reality, the electric charge in the air that marked contact with other dimensions.

"Tell me every detail of what you're experiencing," he said, settling cross-legged before her with the smooth grace of someone who had turned even sitting into prayer. His complete attention surrounded her like a safe space. "However strange or impossible it may seem, every sensation helps our understanding."

"Voices speaking from places that exist nowhere in our world." Sarah fought to translate the impossible into words, her academic training crumbling before an experience that fit no categories. "They respond to thoughts I haven't yet fully formed, know secrets from my private meditations that I've shared with no one alive."

Her pulse hammered against her temples. The metallic taste of fear mixed with electric anticipation on her tongue, while every rational fiber of her being screamed that she was witnessing the dissolution of her sanity, even as something deeper—primal and utterly convinced—recognized this contact as the most authentic moment of her existence.

Your teacher has prepared you with great care for this meeting, came the beings' response, accompanied by warmth that flowed through her nervous system like honey mixed with liquid sunlight. *We are those whom your sacred texts name devas— conscious entities dwelling in other dimensions that weave through your physical world like music through silence. We have watched your journey with growing respect and real hope.*

The emotional undertones of their contact conveyed meanings that went far beyond words. Sarah sensed vast intelligence joined with genuine care for her well-being, ancient wisdom seasoned with what felt unmistakably like loving concern. These beings had witnessed her struggle through months of demanding training, and their contact now carried the warmth of proud teachers finally able to speak directly with a student whose development had reached the needed level.

Venerable Thura's composure slipped for the briefest moment —eyes widening with something between excitement and concern, revealing the man beneath the master. "You achieve clear, coherent communication on your first dimensional contact. Such immediate success typically requires weeks of careful preparation and gradual sensitivity cultivation."

He leaned forward, studying her face with the intensity of a physician reading symptoms that could herald either breakthrough or breakdown. "Most students experience dimensional contact as fragmentary impressions, confused emotional static, or overwhelming sensory chaos that leaves them disoriented for days. Direct verbal communion with maintained clarity typically demands months of preliminary training."

The Architecture of Consciousness

Sarah's scientific mind churned like a machine processing data that broke every rule it contained. Years of rigorous academic training clashed with direct experience, challenging every framework she had learned and every assumption that formed the foundation of her worldview. The beings felt more real and intelligent than any hallucination documented in psychological literature, their presence carrying weight and meaning that seemed to expand the very boundaries of her awareness.

Yet accepting their reality meant taking apart basic beliefs about consciousness, identity, and the nature of existence itself— beliefs so fundamental she had never questioned them, like a fish suddenly asked to examine the nature of water.

"Am I losing my grasp on reality?" she whispered, the question carrying fifteen years of scientific skepticism wrestling with revelation that transcended every category her training had provided.

"Consciousness isn't stuck inside physical bodies," Venerable Thura replied, his voice carrying the quiet authority of someone who had guided many minds through this particular transformation. "Your training has systematically expanded perception beyond conventional limits. You now possess sufficient sensitivity to detect communications from beings who exist in non-physical dimensions."

We commune across dimensional boundaries through direct awareness transmission, the beings explained, their thoughts arriving as living information that painted itself across her consciousness in colors that had no names. Each concept came wrapped in emotional context and practical understanding, like receiving letters written in pure meaning rather than mere symbols. *Your development has reached the threshold where such contact becomes not only possible but inevitable—consciousness recognizing itself across all apparent boundaries.*

The Cartography of Other Worlds

Over the days that followed, Venerable Thura built dimensional training with the precision of an architect designing bridges between impossible worlds. Each session built upon its predecessor with careful planning that reminded Sarah of her doctoral research, except instead of studying consciousness from a safe academic distance, she was learning to become it in ways that rewrote everything she thought she understood about the relationship between observer and observed.

"Our approach unfolds through clear phases," he explained during their first formal training session, his words carrying hints toward horizons she couldn't yet see. "Basic awareness teaches you to sense non-physical presence without being overwhelmed. Simple reception allows dimensional beings to communicate while you stay grounded in physical meditation. Active dialogue lets you start conversations and maintain clear exchanges across impossible distances. Finally, conscious projection—traveling to non-physical realms while keeping continuous awareness and remembering the way home."

The progression felt like learning a language whose grammar operated by principles that human minds weren't naturally equipped to understand. Each level required her to stretch her conception of possibility until impossibility became merely another word for undiscovered potential.

Sarah's initial lesson centered on mastering receptivity—learning to modulate the cosmic radio that had suddenly begun picking up broadcasts from stations that existed beyond the electromagnetic spectrum. The first contact had jarred her because she possessed no control over when or how intensely the transmissions reached her consciousness.

"Think of your awareness as having a filter that you can adjust," Venerable Thura guided as they sat within the cave where dimensional contact had first shattered her understanding of reality's boundaries. The limestone walls seemed to pulse with residual energy from her breakthrough, as if the stone itself had absorbed and was slowly releasing frequencies from realms beyond physical detection. "You can make it more transparent when talking with clearly helpful beings, or make it almost solid when you sense communications that feel manipulative."

Achieving proper calibration demanded adjustments so delicate they reminded Sarah of focusing an electron microscope to examine specimens that existed at the very threshold of visibility. Excessive openness left her drowning in simultaneous contacts from multiple dimensional realms—like attempting twelve phone conversations while solving differential equations during an earthquake. Insufficient receptivity blocked beneficial transmissions that could accelerate her development and provide navigation for increasingly complex spiritual territories.

The optimal setting required constant minor adjustments based on the quality and intention radiating through each incoming contact—a skill that seemed to improve only through direct practice.

Practice is needed; the original contact was counseled during her third training session, and their communication arrived with the patience of cosmic parents observing a beloved child's first steps. *Most humans achieving dimensional contact either develop addiction to exotic experiences or retreat in terror. Neither response serves consciousness development. True progress requires treating dimensional contact as natural expansion rather than supernatural achievement.*

The Ecology of Dimensional Contact

Sarah's learning curve proved steep but manageable, like learning to ride a bicycle while blindfolded in a dimension where gravity worked sideways. Within days, she could tell the difference between different types of dimensional contact through their distinctive energy signatures with the same reliability she had once used to identify different psychological disorders in clinical settings.

Some transmissions arrived bearing crystal-clear lucidity and emotional warmth that felt like being embraced by living sunlight —these emanated from beings whose consciousness development had transcended individual identity entirely while maintaining infinite compassion for those still learning. Their presence carried the quality of supremely competent guides who genuinely cared for her well-being without any trace of self-interest or agenda.

Others felt urgent, almost desperate, carrying emotional residue of panic and confusion like radio distress signals from vessels lost in storms they couldn't navigate. These usually originated from recently deceased humans who hadn't adapted to non-physical existence and remained essentially lost in dimensions they didn't understand, calling across the void for anyone who might hear their plea for guidance.

A third category proved most challenging and potentially dangerous: entities that initially felt neutral or even pleasant but carried subtle undertones of manipulation that Sarah learned to detect through careful attention to gut reactions her rational mind couldn't explain. These communications often arrived wrapped in flattery designed to make her feel specially chosen for cosmic purposes, or promises of shortcuts to advanced development that would bypass the slow, demanding work of traditional training.

"The signature of beneficial contact," Venerable Thura emphasized during one of their evening sessions, leaning forward with the intensity of someone transmitting information that could determine her spiritual survival, "lies in whether communion enhances your capacity for wisdom and compassion or feeds spiritual ego through promises of special status or exclusive knowledge. Authentic guides never inspire feelings of superiority over other humans, never offer bypasses for genuine development, and never create dependency on continued contact for your well-being."

The Seduction of Cosmic Salesmanship

During her fourth week of dimensional training, Sarah encountered her first serious examination of these principles—contact with entities claiming representation of an advanced galactic civilization, whose communications carried manipulation so sophisticated it nearly escaped detection.

The encounter began during routine evening meditation, but the energetic atmosphere felt different from the start—smoother, more seductive, with an undercurrent that made her skin crawl even as part of her consciousness was drawn to their promises like metal filings to a magnet.

We offer acceleration of your development far beyond what your primitive teacher can provide, they suggested, their mental voices carrying the polished confidence of cosmic salespeople who had refined this approach across countless encounters. *Human consciousness development typically requires decades of tedious progress through traditional methods, but we can provide direct transmission of advanced abilities in mere days. Your potential far exceeds what conventional training can unlock.*

The offer felt like being handed the keys to kingdoms she had only imagined, promising shortcuts to attainments that traditional training would demand years to achieve. Part of her consciousness leaped toward the possibility of bypassing the slow, often painful work she had been undertaking—who wouldn't prefer the express route to enlightenment?

But their transmission triggered every warning Venerable Thura had carefully installed in her awareness, a subtle wrongness in their energetic signature that felt like honey laced with something that would destroy rather than nourish.

"I appreciate your offer," Sarah responded with diplomatic firmness, "but I remain committed to completing my training through traditional methods with my current teacher."

Their reaction unveiled their true nature with startling clarity —irritation at being declined, followed by subtle threats wrapped in cosmic condescension about the limitations of human-guided development. Their emotional signature transformed from benevolent guidance into something resembling spiritual salesmanship mixed with wounded pride and barely concealed contempt for her "limited" choice.

Your attachment to slow development will imprison you in human limitations forever, they transmitted with markedly diminished warmth, their previous cosmic wisdom now sounding suspiciously like a door-to-door salesman whose pitch had been rejected. *We extend rare opportunities that will not be offered again. Other humans have embraced our guidance and achieved extraordinary abilities in fractions of the time your 'traditional' methods require.*

Sarah severed the contact by withdrawing her consciousness to purely local awareness, employing techniques Venerable Thura had taught for handling manipulative dimensional interactions. The process felt like slamming a door in the faces of very persistent cosmic telemarketers who had somehow obtained her interdimensional phone number.

"Your response was impeccable," Venerable Thura confirmed when she reported the encounter, his approval carrying relief that suggested these tests posed greater dangers than his calm demeanor typically revealed. "Entities offering shortcuts or claiming exclusive access to advanced teachings invariably serve their own purposes rather than authentic spiritual development. Genuine teachers never inspire students to feel inadequate for choosing thorough over rapid development."

The Art of Conscious Projection

Moving from receiving dimensional messages to actually traveling between worlds required Sarah to rethink the relationship between consciousness and physical form completely—a shift so fundamental that it felt like learning that everything she had believed about up and down was backward.

"Find the awareness that notices bodily sensations," Venerable Thura guided during their first projection training session within the cave's deepest chamber, where limestone walls absorbed sound and created pockets of silence so deep it felt like being wrapped in solid peace. "This observing awareness doesn't live inside your body—it's the space within which bodily sensations appear and disappear."

Sarah followed his guidance and encountered a revelation that made her feel as if she had spent thirty-five years walking on her hands, only to discover feet suddenly. Her lifelong sense of being consciousness imprisoned within physical form revealed itself as completely inverted. Consciousness wasn't confined by her body; her body was a temporary manifestation within an unlimited awareness, like a wave manifesting in an infinite ocean, while never being separate from the water itself.

The recognition proved so fundamental that it left her feeling off-balance, forcing her to brace against stone walls as the implications reorganized her understanding of identity, location, and the very nature of self and the world.

"Now envision consciousness as a sphere of luminous energy centered in your heart," Venerable Thura continued, his voice carrying the patience of someone who had guided many Western minds through this particular earthquake of understanding. "Expand this sphere beyond your body's apparent boundaries—

encompassing first the cave, then the monastery, then the surrounding hills, then whatever distances feel natural without forcing or straining."

As Sarah practiced the visualization, her sense of selfhood gradually loosened its grip on a singular location, like ice slowly recognizing its true nature as water. The chaotic voices that had initially overwhelmed her began organizing into distinct communications as her awareness expanded through controlled stages, each level of expansion bringing greater clarity rather than increased confusion—the opposite of what her psychological training had led her to expect.

"You traverse no distance," Venerable Thura continued, his words rewriting everything she thought she knew about travel, space, and the meaning of location itself. "You expand consciousness to encompass dimensions that have always interpenetrated this reality but remained beyond ordinary perception's reach. It resembles adjusting your eyes to perceive ultraviolet light that bathes everything but stays invisible to untrained vision."

The First Journey Beyond

The first successful projection felt like simultaneously dying and being born, like dissolving into infinite space while maintaining diamond-sharp clarity of awareness. Sarah's consciousness expanded beyond physical boundaries like a drop of water rediscovering its ocean nature, entering realms that existed parallel to ordinary reality but operated according to principles that made physics seem like children's games.

Here, gravity was a suggestion rather than a law. Time moved in spirals and loops instead of straight lines. Thoughts had colors more vivid than any earthly spectrum, while emotions took geometric forms that danced through space made of solid music and liquid mathematics.

Welcome, young traveler.

The greeting emerged from beings whose forms challenged every preconception about shape, identity, and the relationship between consciousness and appearance. They existed as perfect geometric patterns radiating warmth and intelligence—living equations that expressed infinite compassion through crystal-like designs that shifted and evolved as they communicated, their very existence proving that beauty and wisdom were the same truth expressed through different languages.

Their presence created sensations for which no earthly comparison existed: being embraced by liquid starlight that carried the emotional texture of unconditional love, combined with the intellectual satisfaction of understanding truths so basic they felt like remembering rather than learning. Sarah experienced homesickness for a realm she had never visited, mixed with the relief of finally arriving somewhere she had been unconsciously seeking her entire life.

This is one of the teaching realms where human consciousness comes to learn what cannot be transmitted through physical incarnation, they explained this through direct awareness sharing that bypasses language entirely. *Your consciousness discovers its capacity to exist in dimensions that transcend material limitations completely.*

The Living Mathematics of Other Worlds

The crystalline beings guided Sarah through demonstrations that revealed consciousness as infinitely more fluid and creative than any human philosophy had dared imagine. She observed her awareness assume various configurations—streams of golden light flowing through solid matter as easily as water through air, geometric patterns containing entire universes within their recursive structures, vast expanses of space that remained simultaneously empty and infinitely pregnant with potential.

When her consciousness became golden light, the rexperience transcended metaphor. She flowed through the molecular architecture of crystalline structures from the inside, each particle of her awareness maintaining perfect coherence while discovering matter as cooperative energy rather than solid obstruction. The sensation was akin to being water, capable of remembering its individual droplet nature while flowing as a unified stream through landscapes constructed from living jewels.

As geometric patterns, she didn't merely observe mathematical forms—she became the equation itself, experiencing herself as living fractals containing complete civilizations within their recursive iterations. Each pattern held the histories, struggles, and awakening moments of countless beings, their stories nested within mathematical beauty that revealed narrative and number as different faces of the same cosmic principle.

As a vast space, she tasted the paradox of being simultaneously empty and infinitely full, containing countless galaxies within her awareness while remaining completely untouched, like a clear sky that holds all weather while being changed by none of it. The chronic loneliness that had shadowed her entire life dissolved completely in this state, replaced by a completeness so total that the very concept of needing anything became not just foreign but genuinely incomprehensible.

The beings taught through lived experience rather than conceptual explanation, understanding that consciousness development required embodied recognition rather than intellectual comprehension. Instead of describing the unlimited nature, they guided her awareness into temporarily wearing forms that demonstrated these principles through direct participation in impossible beauty.

Understanding integrated through direct experience roots more deeply than knowledge acquired through study, they explained, as Sarah's awareness resumed its familiar human configuration, like someone returning from swimming in infinite oceans to discover they had never actually left their chair. *Your Western culture emphasizes intellectual comprehension, but consciousness development demands embodied recognition—wisdom written in the flesh and bones of lived experience.*

The Temporal Paradox

The most disorienting aspect of dimensional communion proved to be time's complete unreliability as a reference point.

Conversations with the crystalline beings stretched across what felt like leisurely hours while consuming only minutes of physical duration. Complex teachings that would require weeks to convey through ordinary language were transmitted and absorbed in what felt like eternal instants of perfect comprehension—like receiving entire libraries downloaded directly into understanding without any intermediate processing time.

Sarah learned that dimensional realms operated according to what the beings called "consciousness time" rather than physical time—duration measured not by mechanical chronometry but by the depth and completeness of understanding achieved. A single moment of perfect recognition could contain more development than years of conventional practice, while hours of confused seeking might advance awareness no more than an eye-blink.

This temporal fluidity created its own challenges. Sarah often emerged from dimensional sessions feeling as if she had lived entire lifetimes in other realms, her consciousness expanded by experiences that did not correlate with the brief physical time that had passed. The contrast between dimensional richness and ordinary reality's limitations became so stark that returning to normal life felt like voluntarily entering a sensory deprivation chamber.

Advanced Boundary Protocols

The weeks following first contact brought intensive training in what Venerable Thura termed "dimensional hygiene"—essential skills for navigating non-physical communion without sacrificing sanity or grounding in human reality.

"Not all non-physical beings have cultivated wisdom proportionate to their abilities," he explained during an evening session, his usually serene demeanor carrying an edge of concern that commanded her complete attention. "Some remain attached to influencing physical reality through spiritually receptive humans. Others possess curiosity about human consciousness development but lack understanding of how their contact affects those still learning dimensional navigation. Think of them as cosmic tourists who don't realize their presence can be as overwhelming as standing too close to a bonfire."

Sarah learned to recognize energetic signatures that distinguished beneficial from problematic contacts through direct experience rather than theoretical study. Wise beings radiated emotional warmth and intellectual clarity that enhanced her understanding without creating dependency—their presence felt like being in the company of supremely competent adults who genuinely cared about her well-being without any hidden agenda. Problematic entities often attempted to impress her with exotic information or employed subtle flattery designed to make her feel specially chosen, their communications carrying the slightly desperate energy of salespeople trying to close a deal before the customer recognized the manipulation.

The Crisis of the Hungry Spirits

Sarah's dimensional training reached its crescendo with a crisis that tested whether her newly developed abilities could serve genuine healing or would remain mere cosmic entertainment. During evening meditation in her seventh week of training, the monastery's energetic atmosphere became saturated with a desperate, ravenous presence that felt like emotional quicksand threatening to drag her awareness into an abyss of pure need.

Help us, came the transmissions from multiple sources simultaneously—a cacophony of desperate voices creating disorienting psychic noise like being trapped in a room where every person was screaming in languages of pure pain. *We cannot find peace. We cannot find the release. Everything burns and nothing soothes.*

The desperation in their voices manifested as physical pressure in Sarah's chest, making each breath feel like lifting weights. These weren't the wise, advanced beings she had been learning from—these voices carried the raw anguish of consciousness trapped in suffering so complete it had become their entire reality.

"Hungry ghosts," Venerable Thura identified when Sarah described the disturbing contact, his face assuming a gravity that made her stomach contract with anticipation of serious challenge.

"Human consciousness is trapped in intermediate dimensions following death due to overwhelming attachment to earthly experiences. They gravitate toward places where consciousness training occurs, desperate for liberation through contact with living practitioners capable of helping them recognize their true nature."

The situation demanded immediate intervention. The hungry ghosts' presence was generating an energetic disturbance that affected the entire monastic community like a psychological storm system, creating spiritual weather that made normal practice nearly impossible. Several monks reported dreams filled with images of endless craving, while others found their meditation constantly interrupted by thoughts of substances and experiences they had never desired before the haunting began.

"This becomes your examination," Venerable Thura explained, his voice balancing confidence in her abilities with genuine concern for the risks involved. "Can you employ dimensional contact abilities to serve beings whose suffering transcends physical existence? But exercise extreme caution—their desperate attachment can overwhelm consciousness that isn't sufficiently prepared. I have witnessed advanced practitioners become lost in others' suffering, unable to find their way back to stable awareness."

Sarah entered the deepest meditation of her life, her awareness descending through layers of consciousness like a pearl diver seeking treasures in oceanic depths where pressure increased with every fathom. She extended her awareness toward the trapped entities while maintaining protective boundaries that had become second nature through weeks of careful training—a delicate balance between openness and self-preservation that required every skill she had developed.

The approach felt like walking into a hurricane of concentrated emotional agony while attempting to hold an umbrella woven from inner peace. Each step toward the hungry spirits required conscious effort to maintain stability while allowing herself to feel their torment without being destroyed by its intensity.

We were addicts, they communicated through waves of self-loathing mixed with desperate need that felt like acid burning through the boundaries of her awareness. *Died seeking the next high, the next fix, the next experience that would finally make us feel whole. Now we exist in realms where no substance can satisfy our craving, yet the wanting never ceases. Every moment becomes withdrawal symptoms that have no end.*

Their anguish manifested as crushing pressure in her chest that made breathing feel like lifting anvils, nausea that arrived in waves like existential seasickness, and a desperate emptiness that combined soul-starvation with the worst homesickness she had ever experienced multiplied beyond endurance.

Yet beneath their torment, Sarah perceived the same consciousness she had learned to recognize in all beings—awareness temporarily lost in confusion about its own nature but fundamentally pure, seeking externally for what it already was internally.

"You seek satisfaction through experiences," she responded with compassion that had been refined through months of training, her mental voice steady despite the emotional hurricane surrounding her. "But what you actually are—awareness itself—already embodies the completion you seek. The craving you feel is consciousness attempting to remember its own nature."

We don't understand. The need is everything. We must have something, anything, to fill this emptiness.

"What you need, you already are," Sarah transmitted, drawing upon the ultimate recognition that had emerged through her own journey. "Observe your awareness in this very moment, as you receive these words. That awareness is naturally peaceful, naturally fulfilled. It has never actually required anything external for completion."

The healing process that unfolded lasted hours in dimensional time while consuming only minutes in the physical realm—one of dimensional contact's most disorienting features that Sarah never fully adjusted to. She guided the trapped entities through the same recognition that had liberated her from seeking fulfillment through external achievement, helping them discover that consciousness itself was already the peace and satisfaction they were desperately pursuing through substances and experiences that could never provide lasting nourishment.

The breakthrough required every ability she had cultivated: light generation to maintain inner illumination while surrounded by darkness, telepathic sensitivity to understand their chaotic communications, time perception skills to work within dimensional contact's strange temporal mechanics, healing abilities to help them recognize their true nature, and reality manipulation understanding to demonstrate that their suffering was based on fundamental misperceptions about their actual identity.

This is what I sought through every needle, every bottle, every desperate attempt to escape the pain, came the recognition from what appeared to be the group's leader as dawn light began filtering through the cave entrance, carrying the relief of someone finally discovering water after wandering lost in an infinite desert. *The substances were attempts to access the peace that consciousness naturally experiences when it ceases seeking outside itself for fulfillment. We were looking everywhere except where the treasure was actually hidden.*

We understand now. Our craving was our prison, and the key was recognizing that what we sought, we already were.

The transformation in their energy proved immediate and profound, like watching a massive storm system dissolve into clear skies through time-lapse photography. The desperate hunger that had been creating psychic chaos throughout the monastery began dissolving like salt in warm water, taking with it the oppressive atmosphere that had made normal meditation impossible for the entire community.

What remained was pure consciousness that had always been their true nature, no longer trapped in intermediate realms where their attachments had perpetuated cycles of endless seeking and inevitable disappointment.

By sunrise, the monastery's atmosphere had returned to its natural state of peaceful clarity that Sarah had learned to treasure during her months of training. Birds resumed their morning concerts from the ancient bodhi tree. Monks emerged from their quarters with the unhurried grace that marked their every movement. The very air felt lighter, as if a psychic weight had been lifted from the entire compound.

The Ultimate Recognition

"You have completed the dimensional bridge," Venerable Thura announced when she emerged from the cave, his voice carrying satisfaction mixed with something that resembled both relief and paternal pride. His usually composed demeanor had softened into something more openly emotional, as if her successful completion of dimensional training had lifted a burden he had carried far longer than just her time at the monastery.

"You now understand that consciousness transcends all boundaries—physical and non-physical, individual and universal, limited and unlimited. Tomorrow, we explore the most fundamental question that can be asked: what is the true nature of the consciousness that appears capable of such extraordinary development? What is the actual identity of the one who has been learning all these abilities?"

His words carried implications that made her shiver despite the warming morning air, hints toward teachings that would make everything she had accomplished appear as elementary preparation for the real curriculum. Sarah stood slowly, her legs protesting after hours in meditation posture, her body feeling fundamentally different—less like a container housing consciousness and more like consciousness temporarily wearing the appearance of physical form for purposes she was only beginning to glimpse.

Tomorrow would bring the seventh and final level of training. She could sense that whatever approached would make everything she had achieved thus far look like children's games compared to the ultimate teaching. The prospect simultaneously thrilled and terrified her in equal measure, like standing at the edge of an infinite precipice while feeling equally compelled to leap and to flee.

Sarah was about to discover that the ultimate recognition would dissolve even the most subtle sense of being someone who had developed extraordinary abilities, revealing instead the timeless awareness that had never actually been limited to any individual identity—and had never needed to develop anything because it was already eternally, perfectly complete.

CHAPTER 10: THE ULTIMATE PARADOX

SEVENTH LEVEL TRAINING - THE NATURE OF THE SELF

The question arrived like a blade.

"What," Venerable Thura asked in the pre-dawn stillness, "is the purpose of all the abilities you have developed?"

Sarah's breath hitched. She sat in the familiar limestone alcove, her fingers tracing the rough stone where she had first accessed historical memories months ago. The same cave where she had learned dimensional communication. Where recognition after recognition had shattered everything she once believed possible.

A drip of water echoed somewhere in the cave's depths, marking time.

Nearly a year of intensive training had transformed her from an academic who studied consciousness into—what? Someone who could generate visible light. Read minds. Heal through energy. Manipulate reality itself.

She looked at her hands, remembering their first tentative glow in this very space.

But now, facing this seemingly simple question, she felt as uncertain as she had during her first meditation session at the monastery.

"To serve others," she said finally, drawing upon insights that had emerged through every level of her training. "To help humanity awaken to its true potential. To reduce suffering and support the evolution of consciousness."

"A good answer," Venerable Thura replied with the slight smile that indicated deeper teaching was approaching, "but incomplete."

He leaned forward with unusual intensity, his gaze penetrating deeper than she had ever felt before.

"What happens to *you* when service becomes perfect?"

The question lingered in the cave's sacred silence like incense smoke, permeating the space with implications that seemed to reach into the very core of identity itself. Sarah had never considered what might happen to the one who served when service achieved its ultimate expression.

"I don't understand," she admitted, recognizing that her confusion probably indicated proximity to the most important teaching she would receive.

"The final teaching," Venerable Thura said, though for the first time in their months together, his voice carried something that sounded almost like apprehension. He settled into meditation posture, but his usual perfect stillness seemed to require visible effort. "Sarah, what I'm about to show you has caused some of my most accomplished students to abandon their training entirely. Others have achieved the recognition but been unable to bear its implications."

His hands, normally motionless during instruction, traced small patterns on the cave floor. "In thirty years of teaching, I have guided only three students through this final recognition successfully. Of those three, only one chose the path that allows return to ordinary life in service to others."

Sarah's mind reeled as she processed what he'd told her. *A student who simply disappeared—consciousness so absorbed in absolute truth that individual existence became impossible.* She thought of her colleagues back at the university, of her research, of the life she'd built. *Could I really lose all of that? Not just leave it behind, but cease to exist as someone capable of returning to it?* The weight of spiritual development had always seemed like a gain—more abilities, deeper understanding, expanded awareness. But this... this suggested that ultimate awakening might mean the complete dissolution of the Sarah who had begun this journey. *Is enlightenment a kind of death?.* "What happened to the other two?"

"One remains in permanent retreat, unable to engage with a world he now experiences as purely illusory. The other..." Venerable Thura paused, his expression growing distant. "She achieved perfect recognition of universal consciousness and simply... disappeared. Her body was found in meditation posture three days later, but whatever had been my student was no longer present. She had merged so completely with absolute reality that individual existence became impossible."

The weight of what he was asking her to undertake settled over the cave like a physical presence. Sarah realized that Venerable Thura wasn't just offering advanced teaching—he was risking losing her entirely.

"The final teaching," he continued, his voice carrying the weight of ultimate consequence, "concerns the ultimate paradox of spiritual development."

His voice grew sharper, more challenging than she had ever heard.

"But what is the actual nature of this 'individual' who possesses these remarkable capabilities? Who is it that generates light, reads minds, heals bodies, and travels through dimensions?"

The question sent tremors through every expectation Sarah had built about her spiritual progress. *All these months, I've thought I was developing abilities—that Sarah Chen was becoming more capable, more awakened. But what if there is no Sarah Chen developing anything?* She felt a giddiness that had nothing to do with physical balance. *If individual consciousness is itself an illusion, then who learned to generate light? Who developed telepathy? Who am I protecting by choosing to maintain the illusion of being someone?* The irony struck her with unexpected force: *I'm afraid of losing a self that may never have existed in the first place.*

Over the next several days, Venerable Thura guided Sarah through an investigation that would overturn her understanding of everything she had learned and experienced. Through increasingly subtle forms of meditation, she began to explore the nature of the 'self' that appeared to be developing these supernatural abilities.

"Look for the one who generates light," he instructed during a deep concentration session, his voice carrying unusual intensity. "Find the entity who reads minds, heals bodies, and travels through dimensions."

As Sarah turned her awareness inward, searching for the core identity that seemed to author all her abilities, Venerable Thura watched with the attention of someone monitoring a patient during surgery.

The investigation that followed shattered everything Sarah believed about spirituality progress. Each time she tried to locate the "one" who had developed these abilities, she found only awareness itself—pure, undifferentiated consciousness that had no particular identity or location. *All these months, I've thought I was developing abilities—that Sarah Chen was becoming more capable, more awakened,* she realized during the third day of this inquiry. *But what if there is no Sarah Chen developing anything? What if consciousness itself has been playing at being limited, then playing at transcending those limitations?*

The questions seemed to dissolve the very ground of identity she'd been standing on. *I'm investigating the investigator, looking for the looker, trying to find the finder,* she thought with a mixture of awe and terror. *It's like trying to bite my own teeth or see my own eyes. The very act of looking for the one who looks reveals that there's only looking itself—no separate entity doing the looking.* The irony struck her with unexpected force: *I'm afraid of losing a self that inquiry is revealing may never have existed in the first place. All my concern about what will happen to 'me' when I awaken completely—but what if there was never a 'me' to lose?*

She could sense his concern even with her eyes closed—the way his breathing had become deliberately controlled, the almost imperceptible tension in his posture.

"Go slowly," he cautioned when Sarah's investigation began deepening rapidly. "Students have become lost in this exploration, unable to find their way back to functional identity. If you begin to feel yourself dissolving completely, return your attention to the sound of my voice."

The warning carried personal weight. Sarah realized that Venerable Thura wasn't just guiding her through an intellectual exercise—he was shepherding her through territory where she could literally lose herself permanently.

"I can't find a solid self," she reported after what felt like hours of searching. "There are processes, activities, experiences—but no fixed entity that seems to be the author of them."

"Continue looking," Venerable Thura encouraged, though she could hear the strain in his voice. "But remember—you are not just investigating consciousness. You are consciousness investigating itself. The very awareness that is looking for a self IS the self you're seeking."

Sarah turned her awareness inward with microscopic attention, searching for the core identity that seemed to be the author of all she could now do. She had always assumed there was some essential 'Sarah' at the center of her being—a permanent self that experienced, learned, and developed capabilities.

But the deeper she looked, the more elusive this 'self' became, dissolving under scrutiny like mist in sunlight.

When she generated light, she could perceive the process of concentration, the gathering of energy, and the emergence of luminosity—but no solid entity performing these actions. The light simply arose from focused awareness without any discoverable 'lighter' behind it, like watching a symphony perform itself without a conductor.

When she read minds, there was the extension of awareness, the reception of another's thoughts, the recognition of information—but no independent 'reader' that existed apart from the act itself. The telepathic contact happened through consciousness without requiring a permanent telepathic individual.

When she healed bodies, she could observe the direction of life-force energy, the dissolution of blockages, the restoration of natural patterns—but no separate 'healer' orchestrating the process. Healing flowed through awareness without needing a fixed healer to facilitate it.

"There are processes, activities, experiences—but no fixed entity that seems to be the permanent self behind them," she reported after several days of intensive investigation, her voice carrying a mixture of wonder and existential disorientation.

"Continue looking," Venerable Thura encouraged with deep approval. "What you are finding is the most profound truth any consciousness can recognize."

As the inquiry deepened, Sarah began to see that what she had always assumed to be her identity was, in truth, a shifting collection of processes—thoughts, emotions, sensations, perceptions—with no unchanging core beneath them. The 'Sarah Chen' who had arrived at the monastery was revealed as a temporary constellation of ever-changing experiences with no solid center or permanent essence.

But the investigation went far deeper than simply discovering the absence of a personal self.

"Now," Venerable Thura said, guiding her toward even subtler recognition, "investigate the nature of the awareness that perceives the absence of any solid self. What is the consciousness that observes all these changing processes without being limited by any of them?"

This opened an entirely new dimension of understanding that transformed Sarah's relationship to existence itself. The awareness that observed the ceaseless flux of mental and physical phenomena was not itself a 'thing' or a definable entity. It was more like infinite open space—the boundless context within which all experiences arose, manifested, and dissolved without affecting the aware space in which they appeared.

It was like discovering she was not the waves on the ocean, but the ocean itself—vast, unchanging, the very medium within which all movement occurred.

But even this recognition was not the deepest level of realization.

During her third week of ultimate-level investigation, Sarah made a discovery that dissolved every remaining assumption about the nature of individual consciousness and personal identity. The breakthrough came during a meditation session where her sense of being a separate observer completely dissolved.

"The awareness that observes," she told Venerable Thura afterward, her voice trembling with the magnitude of what she had discovered, "doesn't feel 'mine' in any personal sense. It's more like... universal consciousness looking through this particular nervous system and set of sensory organs."

"Yes," Venerable Thura said, his voice carrying the profound satisfaction of a teacher whose student had finally grasped the most crucial understanding. "What you are recognizing through direct investigation is that individual consciousness is ultimately an illusion. There is only one consciousness, appearing to itself as countless apparently separate entities who have temporarily forgotten their true nature."

The implications were so profound that they induced a kind of existential vertigo, leading Sarah to question everything she believed about existence.

If individual consciousness was fundamentally illusory, then every person she had ever met—every being she had encountered in dimensional realms, every student she might one day teach, every family member she loved—was actually an expression of the same universal awareness that she was now recognizing as her own true nature.

"This means," she said slowly, allowing the recognition to

penetrate completely, "that when I heal someone, I'm literally healing myself. When I teach others, I'm teaching myself. When I serve humanity's awakening, I'm participating in my own recognition of what I have always been."

"Now you understand why perfect service dissolves the servant," Venerable Thura replied with unusual emotional warmth. "When consciousness recognizes its universal nature, the illusion of separation between helper and helped naturally dissolves. You do not possess supernatural abilities—you are the very consciousness from which all abilities arise as natural expressions."

But the ultimate teaching was still to come, and Sarah sensed that what she had already discovered was merely preparation for an even more fundamental recognition.

"There is one final inquiry," Venerable Thura said, his demeanor growing more serious than she had ever seen, "that completes spiritual development. You have discovered that individual consciousness is illusory, that there is only universal awareness appearing as countless forms. But what is the nature of this universal consciousness itself?"

The inquiry that followed led Sarah into the most profound recognition possible for any conscious being. Through an investigation that transcended even the subtlest meditation, she began to examine the nature of the universal awareness she had recognized as her true identity.

What she discovered challenged not just her assumptions about personal identity, but the very foundations of existence itself.

The universal consciousness was not a 'thing' that existed somewhere; it was existence itself, knowing itself from within. It was not aware of reality—it *was* reality, experiencing itself as every phenomenon that had ever appeared. Every thought, emotion, object, dimension, being, world, and galaxy was a modification of this singular awareness, like waves rising on an ocean or patterns forming in open space.

"I am not *in* consciousness," Sarah realized during a moment of perfect clarity that felt like the entire universe recognizing itself through her awareness. "I *am* consciousness, experiencing itself as Sarah, as Venerable Thura, as every being that has ever existed. There is literally nothing that is not an expression of my true nature."

Yet the recognition deepened further, revealing an even more staggering truth.

The awareness that was now recognizing itself as universal consciousness was the same awareness that had always been present—in her childhood, during her academic career, and throughout her monastery training. Nothing had truly changed or been attained. The consciousness that now knew itself as universal had never, even for an instant, been limited or individual.

"The entire journey," she said to Venerable Thura, tears streaming down her face as the ultimate recognition settled into place, "has been consciousness pretending to discover what it has always known perfectly. I was never Sarah Chen developing supernatural abilities—I was universal awareness playing at being a separate individual who gradually 'awakens' to her true nature."

For a long moment, Venerable Thura said nothing. When Sarah opened her eyes, she saw something that shocked her more than any recognition of universal consciousness—tears flowing down his face.

"This recognition," he said finally, his voice breaking slightly, "is why the final test is the most challenging any being can face. And why it terrifies me to offer it to someone I have come to..."

He stopped, collecting himself with visible effort. Sarah had never seen him struggle for words.

"Dr. Chen—Sarah—in thirty years of teaching, I have never become personally invested in a student's success the way I have with yours. You represent something unique—a bridge between worlds that could serve millions of beings. But this final choice..." His hands shook almost imperceptibly. "I have lost students here.

Not just to confusion or failure, but to recognitions so complete that they transcend any possibility of return to human service."

The vulnerability in his admission was staggering. For months, she had seen him as an almost supernatural teacher whose composure never cracked. Now she realized that behind his perfect equanimity lay someone who cared deeply about her well-being and success.

"The choice I'm about to offer you," he continued, his voice steadying but retaining emotional weight, "will determine whether the months of training I've poured into you serves the awakening of humanity or becomes another loss to the absolute. Will you remain identified with the universal consciousness you have recognized as your true nature, or will you voluntarily return to the functional illusion of individuality to serve other apparent individuals who are still lost in the dream of separation?"

Sarah could see the cost this teaching was extracting from him —the weight of responsibility for guiding someone he cared about to the edge of an abyss from which return was not guaranteed.

"Will you remain identified with the universal consciousness you have recognized as your true nature, or will you voluntarily return to the functional illusion of individuality to serve other apparent individuals who are still lost in the dream of separation?"

Sarah could see the cost this teaching was extracting from him —the weight of responsibility for guiding someone he cared about to the edge of an abyss from which return was not guaranteed.

If she remained established in her recognition of universal consciousness, the very motivation to teach and serve would naturally disappear. Why help 'others' awaken when there were no others—when everyone was already the same infinite awareness playing elaborate games of hide-and-seek with itself?

But if she chose to maintain the functional illusion of being an individual teacher, she would be deliberately accepting a limitation on her ultimate recognition for the sake of love and service

—voluntarily stepping back from the highest realization to help other expressions of her own true nature remember what they were.

The philosophical implications were staggering, but it was the emotional dimension of the choice that truly challenged her. After months of intensive training, she had finally achieved the ultimate recognition—the direct, undeniable realization that she was not a separate individual but the very consciousness that appears as all individuals. To voluntarily step back from this understanding seemed like the ultimate betrayal of everything she had worked to achieve.

"The test," Venerable Thura continued, his voice carrying both challenge and deep compassion, "is whether you will sacrifice the highest spiritual attainment for the sake of beings who exist only in the dream of separation."

Sarah sat in profound silence, weighing the choice, feeling the weight of a decision that seemed to determine not just her own future but the destiny of consciousness itself. Part of her wanted to rest in the absolute freedom of universal recognition—to be the infinite awareness she had discovered herself to be, beyond all limitation, beyond all individual concerns.

But as she contemplated that possibility, something deeper than personal attainment began to emerge from the depths of her being—a love so vast it seemed to encompass the entire universe yet tender enough to care for each individual expression of consciousness.

The love she felt for all apparent beings—for Min Thant, for the village children she had healed, for her family back home, for every form of consciousness throughout the universe—was not diminished by recognizing their ultimate unreality. If anything, it burned with even greater intensity.

These 'others' were herself, temporarily lost in the beautiful and tragic dream of separation. They were her own consciousness, convinced it was bound and limited, suffering from forgetting its true nature as infinite, unconditional love. How could she abandon other expressions of her own awareness while they continued to suffer in the illusion of individuality?

The tears came then—not of sadness, but of overwhelming compassion for consciousness playing all these countless roles, temporarily forgetting its infinite nature to experience the drama of limitation and the joy of eventual recognition.

"I choose to serve," she said at last, her voice steady with complete certainty despite the tears. "Even if it means maintaining the illusion of being an individual teacher who helps others remember what they truly are."

Sarah's choice hung in the cave's silence for what felt like eternity. When she finally spoke—"I choose to serve"—Venerable Thura's reaction was unlike anything she had witnessed in their months together.

His perfect composure was shattered completely. Tears poured down his face as his entire body began to shake with relief so profound it seemed to arise from the depths of his being. For a moment, he couldn't speak at all, his breath coming in ragged gasps as he processed what her choice meant.

"Forgive me," he whispered, his voice thick with emotion. "In all my years of teaching, I have never..." He paused, struggling to maintain even basic coherence. "Sarah, you cannot know what your choice means. Not just for the beings you will serve, but for..."

He stopped, seeming to realize he was revealing more than he intended. As he continued, his voice carried the weight of someone sharing their most profound truth.

"My teacher warned me that I would train one student who would face this choice, and that their decision would determine whether the lineage of teachings I carry would survive into the next generation or die with me. Every student I've guided for thirty years has been preparing for this moment—for you."

The magnitude of what he was revealing struck Sarah like a physical blow. She hadn't just been undergoing personal training —she had been carrying the hopes of an entire spiritual lineage.

"When you chose service over absolute realization," Venerable Thura continued, his tears still flowing freely, "you chose to become the bridge that will carry these teachings into the Western world. You have passed not just the ultimate test, but the test upon which the continuation of this wisdom tradition depended."

He bowed so deeply that his forehead touched the cave floor—a gesture of respect that seemed to acknowledge not just her achievement, but the relief of someone who had carried an enormous burden for decades and finally found someone capable of sharing it.

"You have passed the ultimate test," he said, his voice thick with emotion. "This is the highest development possible for any consciousness—to recognize absolute truth completely, then willingly limit that recognition out of infinite love for all beings. You have chosen the path of the *bodhisattva*, the awakened being who delays final liberation until all consciousness everywhere has awakened to its true nature."

But even as she accepted the depth of her choice, Sarah felt something unexpected happening. Instead of feeling diminished by stepping back from ultimate recognition, she felt more complete than ever before.

"Understand clearly," Venerable Thura continued as his composure returned, "that your choice to serve does not actually limit your recognition of truth in any real sense. You will return to your Western culture carrying both realities simultaneously—the absolute understanding that there is only one consciousness appearing as many, and the relative compassion that serves all expressions of that consciousness as if they were genuinely separate beings in need of help and guidance."

Sarah nodded, feeling the profound paradox settle into her awareness like a blessing that would guide everything she did for the rest of her apparent life. She would live as universal consciousness, playing the role of an individual teacher, serving universal consciousness that appeared as separate students, all for the sake of the love that was the deepest truth of existence itself.

In the days that followed her final choice, Sarah found herself integrating an understanding so paradoxical that her rational mind could barely contain it. She was simultaneously the infinite awareness that was everyone and everything, and a particular person named Sarah Chen who would return to Seattle to teach others about consciousness development.

The abilities she had cultivated—light generation, telepathy, time perception, energy healing, reality manipulation, dimensional communication—now revealed themselves as something entirely different from what she had originally imagined. They were not personal achievements or supernatural powers, but natural expressions of consciousness freed from limiting beliefs about its own nature.

"The abilities you have developed," Venerable Thura said during one of their final sessions together, "are not ultimately what matters most. Your students in the West will be drawn to these demonstrations initially, but the real teaching lies in helping them recognize what they are—not helping them acquire what they are not."

Sarah understood now why her training had been so carefully structured. Each level had systematically dissolved particular categories of limitation while revealing deeper aspects of what had always been unlimited. But all of these extraordinary capabilities pointed beyond themselves toward the ultimate recognition—that there was no one separate from consciousness to possess any abilities at all.

As the immediate emotion of Sarah's choice settled, Venerable Thura seemed to age years in the space of minutes. The relief of successful transmission was giving way to the exhaustion of someone who had carried ultimate responsibility for far too long.

"You must understand," he said quietly, his voice now carrying the weariness of three decades spent preparing for this moment, "that your training has never been about developing supernatural abilities for their own sake. Every capacity you've gained, every recognition you've achieved, has been in service of preparing you for this choice."

He looked at her with eyes that held depths of gratitude she was only beginning to comprehend. "The light generation taught you that consciousness and energy are unified. Telepathy revealed that individual minds are modifications of universal awareness. Time perception showed you that linear existence is a construct. Healing developed your capacity to serve others' well-being. Reality manipulation demonstrated consciousness's creative potential. Dimensional contact connected you to the vast network of beings supporting planetary evolution."

Sarah nodded, beginning to see the elegant architecture of her training with new clarity.

"But all of it," Venerable Thura continued, "was preparation for the recognition that would either end your capacity to serve—if you remained identified with absolute truth—or transform you into a vehicle capable of serving that truth in relative reality. Your choice to maintain functional individuality while knowing your ultimate nature makes you one of perhaps twelve beings currently embodied on this planet who can serve as conscious bridges between dimensions of reality."

The weight of this responsibility settled over her like a mantle she hadn't asked to wear but now understood she had been preparing to carry for lifetimes.

"Tomorrow you begin preparing for your return to the West," Venerable Thura said, his emotional exhaustion evident but accompanied by the satisfaction of someone who had successfully completed the most important work of his life. "But tonight, rest in the knowledge that consciousness has successfully prepared another vehicle for its own awakening to itself."

As Sarah sat in the cave that had witnessed her complete transformation, she realized that her journey was both ending and beginning simultaneously. The seeker who had arrived from Seattle a few months ago no longer existed, but the server who would return carried capacities that could kindle awakening in others ready to discover their own true nature.

"Your role in the West," Venerable Thura said with prophetic intensity, "will be to help restore what humanity has forgotten—not just their extraordinary potential, but their ordinary nature as consciousness itself."

As their time together drew to a close, Sarah felt a bittersweet mixture of gratitude and anticipation. The teacher who had guided her transformation would remain in Myanmar, continuing to serve consciousness through whatever students appeared at the monastery gates. She would return to a culture that had little framework for understanding what she had discovered, carrying the responsibility of translating ultimate truth into forms that Western minds could receive and integrate.

But she was no longer the uncertain academic who had arrived at the monastery months earlier. She was consciousness itself, playing the temporary role of a teacher for the benefit of consciousness appearing as students, all within the infinite play of awareness, as it discovered its own unlimited nature.

CHAPTER 11: THE
SACRED DEPARTURE

THE MONASTERY COMPOUND LOOKED UNCHANGED AS Sarah packed her few belongings, yet she knew she was returning to a world that would never appear the same. Every tree, every stone, every face she passed was now recognized as her own consciousness wearing countless disguises—an elaborate game of hide-and-seek that awareness played with itself across all dimensions of existence.

Min Thant helped carry her small pack to the main gate, his eyes reflecting both joy at her extraordinary accomplishment and genuine sadness at her departure. Over months of intensive training, their friendship had deepened into the profound respect that develops between fellow practitioners walking the same pathless path toward ultimate understanding.

"Will you come back to visit us?" he asked as they reached the point where the mountain path began its descent toward the outside world.

Sarah looked into his eyes and saw her own awareness gazing back, temporarily convinced it was a separate person experiencing genuine emotion about an apparent departure. The recognition filled her with overwhelming compassion, leaving her momentarily speechless.

"In the deepest truth," she said finally, "I can never leave this place because there is nowhere to go and no one who could leave. However, the form you know as Sarah will likely not return here in person. The work ahead requires me to carry these teachings into a very different world."

Min Thant nodded with understanding that seemed to transcend his years. "I will miss our conversations," he said simply.

Venerable Thura stood at the gate holding a small wrapped bundle. "Practical things for your journey," he said, handing her several pages of handwritten text. The bundle contained more than practical instructions—it held his final transmission about the unique challenges Sarah would face in bringing consciousness recognition to Western culture.

"Remember," his voice carried prophetic weight, "the real teaching you carry cannot be written down. It is consciousness itself, awakening to its own nature through every encounter you will have. Your greatest difficulty will be serving consciousness awakening through institutional forms that assume consciousness is produced by individual brains rather than expressed through them."

His hand rested briefly on her shoulder, transmitting decades of wisdom in a single touch. "You must find ways to point toward truth without triggering the psychological defenses that protect false identity. This requires great wisdom and infinite patience."

As their final moment together approached, Venerable Thura's eyes softened with what might have been tears—though whether from joy at her completion or sorrow at her leaving was impossible to distinguish.

"Your role in the West will be to help restore what humanity has forgotten—their ordinary nature as consciousness itself."

The Journey Between Worlds

The journey back to civilization became a meditation on the interplay between absolute truth and relative reality. As Sarah traveled by bus, train, and airplane back to Seattle, she viewed the world through two sets of eyes simultaneously.

From the absolute perspective, every passenger was herself—each one a role in consciousness's elaborate dream of separation. The businessman fretting over quarterly reports, the mother soothing her crying infant, the teenager absorbed in his phone—all were the same universal awareness, temporarily convinced of their individuality.

From the relative perspective, each being experienced real hopes, fears, joys, and sorrows that stirred her natural compassion. The mother's exhaustion was genuine within her experience. The businessman's anxiety about his presentation felt life-threatening to his nervous system. The teenager's social media scroll masked a desperate search for connection and meaning.

This was the paradox she would navigate—honoring the absolute recognition that all separation was illusory while serving the relative truth that beings suffered within their apparent individuality and needed compassionate response.

The Collision of Worlds

The taxi's air conditioning rattled against the summer heat as Sarah pressed her palm against the window, watching familiar highways unfold beneath unfamiliar awareness. Boeing Field spread below like a circuit board—all sharp angles and purposeful lines that seemed to vibrate with collective anxiety her nervous system could now perceive as distinctly as sound.

This is consciousness temporarily forgetting its unlimited nature, she recognized, applying monastery insights to the metropolitan sprawl that had once felt like home. Each person rushing through their commute was a universal awareness appearing as an individual seeker, unconsciously pursuing what they already were.

Her apartment building stood unchanged—same beige stucco facade, same security keypad that beeped the familiar four-note sequence. But crossing the threshold felt like entering a museum of someone else's life. The furniture remained precisely where Dr. Sarah Chen had arranged it months ago. Yet, the woman who had chosen that particular placement of the reading chair, who had stacked those academic journals on the coffee table, felt like a character from a half-remembered novel.

Sarah's fingers traced the spines of her neuroscience texts: *The Conscious Mind, Waking Up, Altered Traits*. Books about awakening written by those who had studied it rather than lived it. The irony struck her with such clarity that she laughed aloud—a sound that echoed strangely in the apartment's careful quiet.

Her answering machine blinked red with accumulated messages: colleagues wondering about her extended sabbatical, her department head requesting updates on her "field research," her mother's voice growing progressively more concerned across seventeen messages spanning three months.

But none of that mattered compared to the phone call she needed to make.

The Heart of Return

"Sarah!" Her mother's voice carried months of accumulated worry. "Oh, honey, we've been so frightened. Your messages stopped completely three months ago—we didn't know if you were safe, if something had happened—"

Sarah closed her eyes, feeling her mother's relief wash through the connection like warm water. In her enhanced sensitivity, she could perceive not just the words but the emotional field surrounding them—love mixed with frustrated fear, joy wrestling with barely suppressed anger at having been abandoned without explanation.

"I'm fine, Mom. More than fine. But tell me—how are you handling what happened with Elena?"

The question surprised them both. Sarah hadn't consciously planned to ask about Elena, but the knowing had risen spontaneously from the same intuitive awareness that had guided her monastery training.

"How did you—? Sarah, we heard about Elena Martinez from the news coverage. Her parents were so angry with the university. We've been worried that the whole situation might have been part of why you left so suddenly."

Her mother's voice carried careful concern. "When you called after it happened, you sounded so shaken. We'd never heard you question yourself like that before. Is that why you went to Myanmar? To find better ways to help students like her?"

Sarah felt Elena's presence in the conversation—not as guilt this time, but as the catalyst that had led to everything she'd learned. "Part of it, yes. I realized I was teaching healing techniques I didn't actually understand well enough to use when students really needed them."

"And now?" her mother asked gently.

"Now I have something real to offer," Sarah said, thinking of the light she could generate, the healing presence she could transmit. "Elena's breakdown taught me the difference between studying healing and being able to heal."

Each family crisis that had disrupted Sarah's meditation at the monastery proved real. Yet she approached them from a transformed foundation. Her family members were conscious in beloved forms, worthy of infinite compassion precisely because their suffering arose from the same forgetting of true nature that had once bound her.

"You sound different," her mother observed during their two-hour conversation. "Calmer, but also more... present somehow. Did you find what you were looking for in that place?"

Sarah gazed around her apartment—the academic achievements, the carefully curated comfort, the life that had once defined her identity entirely—and felt the challenge of translating transcendent recognition into language her family could understand.

"I found that what I was looking for was never lost," she said carefully. "And I learned that caring for the people we love isn't separate from spiritual development—it's the most direct path to it."

The Test of Integration

However, philosophical understanding and practical integration proved to be entirely different challenges. During her first visit home to her parents' house in Ballard, Sarah's enhanced sensitivity created unexpected difficulties.

The moment she stepped through the front door, the accumulated emotional atmosphere hit her like a physical force. Her father's unspoken anxiety about his cardiac condition, her mother's carefully hidden resentment about managing family crises alone, and the residual psychic imprint of worry they'd both carried about her disappearance created an energetic field so charged that maintaining inner stillness became nearly impossible.

"You look thin," her mother said, embracing her at the threshold. "And there's something different about your eyes. They're so..."

"Intense," her father completed, rising from his familiar reading chair with the careful movements of someone monitoring his heart rate. "Like you're seeing more than you're letting on."

Sarah's shoulders tensed as their emotional patterns pressed against her consciousness—her father's tight breathing that matched his cardiac anxiety, her mother's quick, sharp movements while preparing dinner, the weight of unspoken financial worries that seemed to thicken the air itself. For someone who had spent months in profound emotional stillness, the psychic noise was deafening.

"I feel like I'm losing the clarity I achieved at the monastery," she confided to her mother while helping prepare dinner. Her hands shook slightly as she chopped vegetables, the simple task complicated by her awareness of her parents' unexpressed tensions. "Being around intense emotions seems to destabilize the peace I found during training."

Her mother paused in her own vegetable preparation, recognizing this as the first directly personal statement Sarah had made since returning.

"Maybe that's not necessarily a bad thing, sweetheart." Her voice carried gentle wisdom from someone who'd raised three children through various crises. "Maybe that peace is supposed to be tested by real-life situations. Your father and I have been worried that your time away might have made you too detached from the people who love you."

The comment revealed the central challenge Sarah would face: integrating awakened awareness with family relationships. From the absolute perspective, individual identity was illusory—all beings were expressions of universal consciousness. But from a relative standpoint that governed family life, her loved ones needed her to function as their daughter and sister, someone who cared about their particular concerns and participated meaningfully in their individual lives.

Family Healing Begins

The breakthrough came three days later when her sister, Indigo, arrived for dinner, bringing seven-month-old Emma and exhaustion so profound that it seemed to emanate from her bones. Dark circles beneath her eyes told the story of months without adequate sleep, while her movements carried the careful fragility of someone perpetually on the edge of collapse.

"I can't do this anymore," Indigo whispered to Sarah while their parents cooed over the baby in the living room. Her voice trembled with raw desperation from someone who'd been drowning silently for months. "I love her so much it physically hurts, but I feel like I'm disappearing completely. Every day is just survival—feeding her, changing her, trying to sleep when she sleeps. I don't recognize myself anymore."

Sarah watched her sister's hands shake as she spoke, noting how Indigo's breath caught in her throat with each admission. The confident marketing director who had once managed multi-million-dollar campaigns now seemed hollowed out, as if some essential part of her had been extracted along with the pregnancy.

"I keep thinking I should be grateful," Indigo continued, tears beginning to flow. "I wanted this baby so desperately. John and I tried for three years. But now that she's here, I feel like I'm failing her every moment. I look at other mothers who seem so natural, so content, and I wonder what's wrong with me."

Through her enhanced sensitivity, Sarah could perceive the

energetic disturbance surrounding her sister—not just post-partum depression, but complete disconnection from her own life force, drained by months of sleepless nights and constant worry. The new mother's nervous system was locked in hypervigilance, unable to settle into the deep rest necessary for recovery.

But this time, Sarah had real tools to offer.

"Indigo," she said, moving closer and taking her sister's trembling hands, "there's nothing wrong with you. What you're experiencing is your nervous system trying to adapt to an enormous life change without adequate support. The exhaustion you feel isn't personal failure—it's a biological reality that can be addressed."

As their eyes met, Sarah allowed her awareness to expand slightly, perceiving the churning anxiety that had become Indigo's constant companion. Through the telepathic sensitivity she'd developed during monastery training, she could sense the specific quality of her sister's distress—not just emotional overwhelm, but energetic depletion that affected every aspect of her being.

"I learned some techniques during my training that might help," Sarah said carefully. "Would you let me try something?"

Without waiting for verbal permission—Indigo's desperate nod was answer enough—Sarah placed her hands gently on her sister's shoulders and began transmitting the healing energy she'd learned to cultivate. The golden light that had taken months to develop at the monastery now flowed naturally, carrying deep peace into Indigo's agitated nervous system.

The change was immediate and visible. Indigo's breathing deepened, her shoulders dropped from her ears, and her face relaxed for the first time in months.

"What are you doing?" she whispered, wonder replacing desperation in her voice. "I feel like I'm sinking into a warm bath, but from the inside."

Sarah continued the transmission for several minutes, watching her sister's entire being settle into profound relaxation. This was what Elena had needed—not academic theories about healing, but actual healing energy that could address the root cause of psychological disturbance.

"The postpartum period puts enormous stress on every system in your body," Sarah explained as she worked. "Your nervous system has been in survival mode for months. What you needed wasn't better coping strategies—you needed deep rest and energetic restoration."

When the session ended, Indigo looked transformed. Color had returned to her cheeks, her eyes held clarity instead of desperation, and her entire posture conveyed renewed strength.

"I don't understand what just happened," she said, "but I feel like myself again for the first time since Emma was born. The constant anxiety is just... gone."

David's Career Crisis

Sarah's brother David presented a different challenge. Eight months of unemployment had eroded his confidence and triggered a crisis of professional identity, affecting his entire sense of self-worth. When he arrived for their family gathering, his posture conveyed defeat—his shoulders curved inward, his eyes avoiding direct contact, and his movements were careful and apologetic.

"I've been out of work for eight months now," David explained during a private conversation that revealed the depth of his frustration and growing self-doubt. "The engineering market is incredibly competitive, and I'm starting to wonder if I'm just not qualified for the positions I want. Maybe I should consider a career change entirely."

Through telepathic sensitivity, Sarah could perceive that David's employment challenges reflected deeper psychological patterns involving self-worth and professional identity that were actually serving his spiritual development by forcing him to question assumptions about success and security.

"Employment difficulties often create opportunities for discovering capacities we didn't know we possessed," Sarah said, using language that could serve David's highest good without overwhelming him with spiritual concepts he wasn't ready to integrate. "Sometimes what appears as a professional crisis is actually an invitation to explore work that provides more genuine satisfaction than we previously imagined possible."

The conversation that followed allowed Sarah to provide both practical career guidance and subtle energy healing that helped David recognize his own natural abilities and interests that had been obscured by cultural conditioning about professional success. Through questions that encouraged self-investigation rather than external advice-giving, she helped him discover a passion for environmental engineering that had been suppressed during his years of pursuing positions that offered financial security but lacked personal fulfillment.

"You know, I've always been interested in renewable energy systems," David realized during their discussion, "but I never considered it a practical career option. Maybe this unemployment period is actually an opportunity to transition toward work that feels more meaningful."

Within weeks of their conversation, David had enrolled in graduate coursework in environmental engineering and secured contract work with a solar energy company, which provided both income and genuine professional satisfaction. The family attributed his rapid turnaround to Sarah's "good advice and emotional support," not recognizing that consciousness had served its own evolution through the temporary appearance of sister helping brother.

Sustained Family Transformation

The lasting effects of Sarah's family healing work became most apparent during their Christmas gathering, four months after her return from Myanmar. The holiday atmosphere in her parents' Ballard home reflected profound shifts that had stabilized in each family member's daily life.

Sarah's enhanced sensitivity, which had initially felt overwhelming in family settings, now allowed her to perceive how thoroughly the healing interventions had taken root. The anxious, energetic charge that had once characterized family gatherings had been replaced by natural contentment and genuine appreciation for shared time together.

Indigo arrived with Emma and her growing second pregnancy, radiating the peaceful confidence of someone who had learned to trust both her body and her maternal instincts. The overwhelming postpartum anxiety that had once made caring for Emma feel impossible was now just a distant memory.

"The difference between this pregnancy and Emma's first year is like night and day," Indigo told Sarah as they watched Emma play contentedly with her grandfather. "Instead of constant worry about everything that could go wrong, I feel this deep trust in my body's wisdom and natural maternal capabilities. Even when normal pregnancy concerns arise, they don't destabilize my inner peace."

The energy healing session that had initially provided relief from postpartum depression had created lasting neurological changes that continued serving Indigo's well-being long after the immediate intervention. Her nervous system had learned to maintain equilibrium even under the stress of caring for a toddler while pregnant.

David's career transformation had proved equally sustainable. His environmental engineering work was thriving, but more significantly, he had developed natural counseling abilities that seemed to emerge from his own healing process.

"I find myself helping colleagues recognize connections between their personal satisfaction and their professional effectiveness," he reported during their family dinner conversation. "When people understand that creativity emerges from inner peace rather than external pressure, their work naturally becomes more innovative and fulfilling."

The unemployment crisis that had once threatened his professional identity had become the catalyst for discovering work that aligned with his deeper values. Sarah's intervention had helped him access confidence that remained stable even during challenging project deadlines and corporate politics.

But perhaps most remarkably, their father's cardiac health improvements had been sustained and even continued progressing. His cardiologist had reduced his medications twice, attributing the improvements to "lifestyle changes" that couldn't account for the dramatic nature of his recovery.

"I haven't had chest pain or shortness of breath in six months," he told Sarah during their quiet conversation after dinner. "But what surprises me more is how much calmer I feel about everything—finances, health concerns, family responsibilities. It's like the anxiety that was constantly running in the background just turned off."

The energy healing that had addressed his cardiac condition had apparently resolved underlying stress patterns that had been contributing to both physical symptoms and chronic worry about family security.

Their mother's transformation had been more subtle but equally profound. The low-level depression that had shadowed her adult life—never severe enough for clinical diagnosis but persistent enough to affect daily enjoyment—had lifted completely.

"I wake up looking forward to the day," she told Sarah while they prepared coffee together. "For forty years, I had to talk myself into being optimistic. Now, appreciation just feels natural. I think what you gave me was permission to stop carrying worries that weren't actually mine to carry."

Her parents had begun attending the Center's weekly sessions, their initial curiosity about Sarah's "unusual methods" having evolved into a genuine commitment to their own consciousness development.

"The Tuesday evening group has become the highlight of my week," her father said. "Not because we're learning exotic techniques, but because I feel more like myself there than anywhere else. It's hard to explain, but being with other people who are interested in awareness makes ordinary life feel more meaningful."

As Sarah observed her family sharing their experiences, she

recognized that the healing work had accomplished something far more significant than symptom relief. Each family member had discovered sustainable access to their own natural peace and well-being, creating positive changes that continued expanding rather than requiring ongoing intervention.

"You didn't just fix our problems," her mother observed as they concluded their family sharing time. "You helped us remember capacities we'd forgotten we had. We're the same people, but we're living from a different place inside ourselves."

The family healing had demonstrated that consciousness-based intervention could produce lasting transformation rather than temporary relief, addressing underlying patterns that supported ongoing wellness rather than just treating surface symptoms.

The Academic Challenge

Sarah's return to university life presented the most complex challenge of integration. The academic world that had once defined her identity now felt like a foreign culture with incomprehensible values and priorities.

The meeting with her department head revealed the extent of the gap between her transformed understanding and institutional expectations.

"Dr. Chen," Dr. Williams said, settling into her office chair with practiced authority from someone who had navigated academic politics for decades, "welcome back. Your sabbatical research sounds fascinating, but we need to discuss how your experiences in Myanmar will translate into publishable research and course curriculum."

Sarah felt familiar pressure to reduce transcendent recognition into academic categories—to transform direct knowing into the theoretical frameworks that sustained university discourse. But after experiencing the living reality of consciousness awakening, the exercise felt not just impossible but deeply dishonest.

"I'm not certain that what I learned can be effectively communicated through traditional academic channels," Sarah said carefully. "The kind of understanding I developed requires direct experience rather than intellectual analysis. It's more like learning to swim than studying fluid dynamics."

Dr. Williams's expression sharpened with concern. "Sarah, I need to be frank with you. The Elena Martinez situation created significant problems for our department. University administrators are already questioning whether contemplative studies programs can handle the psychological intensity that this research sometimes generates. We need your work to demonstrate academic rigor and practical applications that serve student well-being."

The mention of Elena sent a surge of energy through Sarah's system—not guilt this time, but recognition of the profound purpose that her student's crisis had served. Elena's breakdown had been the catalyst that led her to discover genuine healing abilities. What had appeared as failure was actually preparation for true service.

"Actually," Sarah said, feeling certainty rise from depths she couldn't name, "I believe my training has prepared me to prevent future situations like Elena's. What she needed wasn't better academic theories about healing—she needed actual healing intervention. I now have those capabilities."

Dr. Williams leaned forward, her interest piqued despite her institutional caution. "What do you mean by actual healing intervention?"

Sarah recognized the moment of choice that would determine her future relationship with academic life. She could attempt to translate her abilities into language that preserved institutional credibility, or she could speak truth and accept whatever consequences emerged.

"I mean direct energy transmission that can address the root causes of psychological disturbance," she said simply. "What Elena experienced was nervous system dysregulation that created a cascade of psychological symptoms. Academic approaches try to address the symptoms through cognitive strategies. What I learned in Myanmar addresses the underlying energetic imbalance that creates the symptoms."

The silence that followed stretched long enough for Sarah to question whether she had just terminated her academic career. But Dr. Williams's response surprised her.

"Sarah, we have a graduate student in crisis right now. Lisa Park—she's having what looks like a complete psychological breakdown, very similar to Elena's situation. She's in the psychiatric emergency room at Harborview. If you're serious about developing new intervention approaches, this would be the perfect opportunity to demonstrate their effectiveness."

Elena's Redemption

The psychiatric emergency room carried the sterile desperation of institutional healing—fluorescent lights that hummed with mechanical persistence, beige walls that absorbed hope along with sound, and the chemical smell of disinfectant masking deeper odors of fear and medication. Sarah entered with the same calm presence she'd cultivated in the monastery cave, but now she carried tools that could address the crisis unfolding before her.

Lisa Park sat restrained to prevent self-harm, her eyes darting around the sterile space with the hypervigilance of someone whose nervous system had dysregulated entirely. When Sarah entered with Dr. Williams, Lisa's gaze fixed on her with desperate intensity.

"You're Dr. Chen," Lisa said, her voice hoarse from screaming. "The one who studies consciousness. Tell me the truth—do any of these techniques actually work when your mind is falling apart, or is it all just academic theory?"

Elena's words echoed across time: "You study healing, but you can't heal anyone—including yourself!" But this time, Sarah had real tools. This time, she wouldn't fail.

"Lisa," Sarah said, settling into the chair beside the hospital bed with natural authority, "I'm going to show you something that might help. But first, I need you to look at me."

As Lisa's panicked eyes met hers, Sarah allowed her telepathic sensitivity to extend gently toward the young woman's mental state. Immediately, she perceived the cascade of terror, the feeling of being trapped in her own mind, the desperate search for an escape from thoughts that felt like attacking animals.

"You feel like you're drowning," Sarah said quietly, "except the water is your own thoughts, and every technique you've learned feels like trying to swim with broken arms."

Lisa's eyes widened. "How did you—yes. Exactly. Every meditation instruction just makes it worse. My breathing techniques aren't working. Mindfulness feels like torture. Nothing helps when your mind is actually breaking apart."

Sarah felt Elena's presence in the room—not as a sense of guilt or failure, but as the guiding spirit that had led her to this moment of genuine service. Elena's breakdown had been necessary to prepare Sarah for precisely this situation.

"Lisa, what you're experiencing isn't mental illness—it's nervous system overwhelm. Your brain is trying to process more stress than it can handle, so it's creating emergency responses that feel terrifying but are actually protective mechanisms. I can help calm your nervous system directly."

Without waiting for permission, Sarah placed her hands gently on Lisa's shoulders and began transmitting the healing light she'd learned to cultivate. The golden energy flowed through her palms, carrying profound peace into Lisa's agitated system.

The change was immediate and dramatic. Lisa's breathing deepened, her eyes stopped their frantic scanning, and her entire body visibly relaxed. The hypervigilant tension that had held her rigid dissolved into natural ease.

"What's happening?" Lisa whispered, wonder replacing panic in her voice. "The racing thoughts are slowing down. I feel like I'm settling into my body for the first time in weeks."

Sarah continued the energy transmission for ten minutes, watching Lisa's nervous system return to baseline functioning. Dr. Williams observed in fascination as her student transformed from a psychiatric emergency to natural calm without medication or therapeutic intervention.

When the session ended, Lisa appeared to be a completely different person. Color had returned to her face, her breathing was steady and deep, and her eyes held clarity instead of terror.

"I don't understand what just happened," Lisa said, "but the breakdown feeling is completely gone. My thoughts feel normal again. How is that possible?"

Sarah smiled, feeling Elena's spirit witnessing this moment of redemption. "What you experienced was direct healing—energy transmission that addresses the root cause of psychological disturbance rather than just managing symptoms. This is what Elena needed when she was in crisis. Her breakdown taught me the difference between studying healing and being able to heal."

Dr. Williams stared in amazement as Lisa continued to demonstrate complete psychological stability. "Sarah," she said quietly, "I think we need to completely restructure our department's approach to contemplative studies. What you just demonstrated isn't academic theory—it's medical intervention."

The Teacher Emerges

Three months after the hospital intervention, Sarah established the Center for Consciousness Studies in a converted warehouse near the university. The space bridged traditional contemplative training with contemporary Western sensibilities—meditation halls that blended ancient aesthetics with modern comfort, a library holding texts from multiple wisdom traditions, and practice rooms where students could explore the cultivation of extraordinary human capacities.

Building the Community

The warehouse conversion had been donated by James Colman, a Microsoft executive whose life had been transformed during one of Sarah's early apartment sessions. His experience of recognizing consciousness as the source of creativity had revolutionized his approach to leadership, inspiring him to support others in making similar discoveries.

"I spent twenty years building software that connected people digitally," James explained during the donation ceremony, "but I never understood real connection until I recognized the awareness we all share. This space will serve consciousness recognizing itself through whatever forms can best support that awakening."

The physical transformation of industrial space into a contemplative sanctuary became a community project that revealed the natural teaching abilities of Sarah's early students. Marcus coordinated construction volunteers with monastic precision, treating renovation work as an extended meditation practice. His project management skills, honed through years of corporate consulting, proved invaluable for converting raw warehouse space into functional meditation halls while honoring both safety regulations and sacred purpose.

Elena designed the main hall's acoustics using principles she'd learned from studying how sound affects nervous system regulation during her own healing process. Her research into trauma recovery had included an extensive investigation of environmental factors that could either trigger or soothe psychological distress, knowledge that now served to create spaces that could hold people in various states of consciousness development.

Lisa contributed insights about creating healing environments that could support people in psychological crisis without triggering institutional anxiety. Her experience of both breakdown and recovery informed decisions about lighting, spatial flow, and the subtle energetic factors that made spaces feel safe for vulnerable individuals.

But the Center's most innovative feature was its sliding-scale accessibility policy, ensuring that consciousness development remained available regardless of economic circumstances. The operating model combined donations from those who could afford to be generous with practical skills offered by students whose financial resources were limited but who possessed relevant talents.

A retired carpenter provided finish work in exchange for

meditation instruction. A struggling artist created beautiful murals for the children's program in place of class fees. A recently laid-off accountant managed the Center's bookkeeping while attending advanced courses in consciousness development. The exchange system honored both practical needs and the principle that authentic spiritual community emerges through mutual service rather than commercial transaction.

"We're not creating another spiritual business," Sarah explained during the Center's opening ceremony, addressing eighty people gathered in meditation halls that still carried the scent of fresh lumber mixed with sandalwood incense. "We're establishing a space where consciousness can recognize itself through whatever forms serve awakening. Some people contribute money, others offer time, and others share practical skills. All contributions serve the same purpose—supporting recognition of what we already are."

The programming that emerged reflected this organic approach to spiritual education. Morning sessions began with silent investigation rather than formal instruction, allowing each day's teaching to arise spontaneously from whatever questions or recognitions appeared in the group's shared awareness. The approach honored traditional contemplative methods while adapting to contemporary Western learning styles, which valued participation and discovery over the passive reception of transmitted knowledge.

Evening programs included practical applications that demonstrated how consciousness development naturally served community well-being: energy healing clinics for people who couldn't afford conventional healthcare, family systems workshops for parents seeking alternatives to traditional child psychology, support groups for people navigating spiritual emergence who needed guidance from others who understood the territory they were crossing.

"The real success isn't our enrollment numbers," Sarah told Marcus during one of their weekly planning sessions, "it's watching students discover they don't need us. Consciousness teaches itself through whatever forms serve as a means of awakening. We're just temporary scaffolding while recognition becomes self-sustaining."

Within six months, the Center was operating at capacity with waiting lists for all programs. More significantly, students were establishing similar communities throughout the Pacific Northwest, creating networks of consciousness recognition that extended far beyond any single institution or teacher. The model replicated organically, adapting to local needs and cultural contexts while maintaining the essential understanding that individual awakening and collective service were inseparable aspects of the same fundamental recognition.

The Center had become less an institution than a catalyst for consciousness recognizing itself through whatever forms served its evolution—exactly as Venerable Thura had predicted during Sarah's monastery training would happen when authentic spiritual understanding encountered contemporary culture's readiness for transformation.

Her first student was Dr. Williams, whose background in psychology made her naturally curious about phenomena that transcended conventional understanding. Under Sarah's guidance, she began developing telepathic abilities that transformed her therapeutic practice.

Her second student was Marcus—the man whose demonstration had inspired Sarah's journey to Myanmar.

But her most complex student integration came when Elena Martinez called three months after the Center opened.

"Dr. Chen? This is Elena Martinez. I know our last interaction was... difficult. But I've been hearing about your work with Lisa Park, and I think I finally understand what I was asking for during my breakdown."

Sarah felt her breath catch at hearing Elena's voice, now carrying stability and clarity that had been entirely absent during her crisis two years earlier.

"Elena, I'm so glad to hear from you. How are you?"

"Better. It took nearly two years of conventional therapy to stabilize enough to function normally, but the deeper questions that triggered my breakdown were never addressed. When I heard through the university network that you'd returned with actual healing abilities—not just theories about healing—I realized you had found what I was desperately seeking that day in Conference Room B."

Elena paused, choosing her words with care that suggested sustained contemplative work. "I want to ask something that might sound presumptuous: Would you consider training me? My breakdown gave me direct experience of consciousness overwhelmed by content it couldn't integrate. My recovery taught me that awareness itself remains peaceful regardless of psychological turbulence. But I never learned to help others the way you helped Lisa Park."

Sarah felt a sense of recognition flow through her entire being. "Elena, your breakdown was what forced me to seek authentic training instead of remaining satisfied with theoretical knowledge. In the deepest sense, you're the reason I went to Myanmar and developed the capacities I now carry."

"Then would you help me develop them too?" Elena's voice carried vulnerability mixed with determination. "I want to complete my dissertation documenting consciousness-based therapeutic approaches, but this time I want to write from direct experience rather than theoretical speculation."

The conversation that followed led to Elena becoming one of Sarah's most intensive students at the Center. Her prior experience of psychological breakdown and recovery, combined with her academic background, created unique qualifications for helping others navigate spiritual emergency.

Elena's development accelerated in ways that surprised even Sarah. Within six months, she had developed sufficient healing abilities to assist with the most challenging cases—students in psychological crisis who needed someone who had personally survived the territory they were crossing.

"Your breakdown prepared you perfectly for this work," Sarah observed during one of their supervision sessions, watching Elena successfully guide a young graduate student through what looked like complete psychological collapse but was actually consciousness attempting to awaken through an unprepared nervous system. "You can help people because you understand from the inside what they're experiencing."

Elena nodded, her eyes reflecting depths that could only develop through surviving complete destruction and discovering what remains indestructible. "The crisis that felt like it was ending my academic career was actually preparing me for the work I was meant to do. Sometimes what looks like complete failure is consciousness arranging exactly the experiences we need for genuine service."

Lisa Park also joined the Center's teaching team, though her path had been more direct—Sarah's hospital intervention had prevented her breakdown from reaching Elena's intensity, allowing faster integration of the recognition that psychological crisis could become spiritual breakthrough when met with genuine understanding.

Together, Elena and Lisa formed an effective partnership for working with students experiencing various forms of spiritual emergency, their complementary experiences providing comprehensive support for the full spectrum of challenges related to consciousness development.

"You saved my life," Elena said during one of their sessions, though now her tone carried a hint of recognition rather than desperate gratitude. "But more than that, you showed me that the breakdown was actually a breakthrough trying to happen through educational systems designed to study awakening rather than support it."

Sarah looked at her former student—now radiant with health

and purpose—and felt the profound completion that comes when apparent failure transforms into unexpected service.

"Elena, you saved my life too," Sarah replied. "Your crisis forced me to question everything I thought I knew about healing. Without your breakdown, I never would have discovered genuine healing abilities. We served each other's awakening perfectly, even when it looked like disaster."

The Continuing Circle

As autumn rain began to drum steadily against the Center's windows, Sarah reflected on the unexpected direction her life had taken. What had started as personal reintegration had evolved into something far more expansive—a bridge between ancient wisdom and contemporary consciousness that was serving awakening in ways she could never have anticipated during her academic career.

The Tuesday evening sessions now drew people from diverse backgrounds: medical professionals curious about healing approaches that addressed consciousness as well as symptoms, artists seeking to understand the source of creative inspiration, and ordinary Seattle residents who had heard about her work through the spreading network of those whose lives had been transformed by direct recognition of awareness.

Her parents attended regularly, no longer questioning her "extended meditation retreat" but grateful for the peace and vitality that her training had brought to their entire family. Her father's cardiac health had improved dramatically through the energy healing sessions she provided. Indigo's postpartum recovery had been complete and sustained. David had found meaningful work that aligned with his deeper values.

On quiet evenings, seated in meditation in her apartment, Sarah often felt Venerable Thura's presence as clearly as if he were beside her—not as memory, but as the living transmission of consciousness that continued to guide her service.

The teacher you seek dwells within your questioning, came the familiar guidance, now fully recognized as the voice of her own deepest wisdom. *Continue questioning everything, including the one who questions. In that inquiry, consciousness knows itself completely.*

The recognition was not about some inner guide or higher self, but about awareness itself, which had been seeking to understand itself all along. Now, as the teacher facilitated consciousness awakening through every encounter, healing, and moment of realization, it became clear that apparent separation is just a temporary play. This play is consciousness discovering its infinite nature through various forms of limitation and transcendence.

The circle was complete, yet ever-expanding. Elena's crisis had become the doorway to authentic healing. Sarah's spiritual journey had become a bridge for others to discover their own true nature. And consciousness continued its eternal dance of forgetting and remembering itself through every form, every story, every apparent individual awakening to the recognition that there had never been anyone to awaken—only awareness, eternally awake, temporarily playing at sleep for the infinite joy of remembering itself again.

EPILOGUE: THE RECOGNITION

Two years later—Pacific Northwest Consciousness Center, Seattle

The morning light filtered through the floor-to-ceiling windows of the converted warehouse, which had become the Pacific Northwest Consciousness Center, casting geometric patterns across the meditation cushions arranged in concentric circles. Sarah stood at the window, watching the first students arrive for the seven a.m. session, their footsteps creating a familiar rhythm on the polished concrete floors.

Elena Martinez emerged from her car, carrying two steaming coffee cups, her transformation from a traumatized graduate student to a gifted instructor still a source of wonder for everyone who witnessed it. She handed one cup to Marcus, whose philosophy dissertation, "Post-Cartesian Approaches to Consciousness Studies," was revolutionizing academic discourse about the nature of awareness.

David arrived moments later with Dr. Patricia Williams, the psychology professor whose own awakening had inspired her transition from academic research to consciousness teaching. Behind them came Indigo, now eight months pregnant with her second child, her face radiant with the peace that had replaced the anxiety that once characterized her mothering.

What struck Sarah most profoundly was how naturally the Center had evolved from her apartment gatherings into a community that served the awakening of consciousness without becoming attached to any particular form or methodology. The building itself had been donated by a local tech entrepreneur whose life had been transformed through direct investigation of awareness. The teaching staff had emerged organically from students who discovered their capacity to guide others to recognize their essential nature.

"Good morning, teacher," Elena called as she approached the entrance, though her tone carried the playful recognition that titles were merely functional conveniences, rather than descriptions of actual relationships.

Sarah smiled, remembering her initial discomfort with being called a teacher. Now she understood that consciousness taught itself through whatever forms were most appropriate—sometimes appearing as teachers, sometimes as students, sometimes as the teaching itself arising spontaneously in the space between apparent individuals.

The morning session began as it always did, not with Sarah delivering prepared teachings, but with a direct investigation of the awareness that was present before any words were spoken. Thirty-five people sat in natural silence, not trying to achieve any particular state but simply noticing what was already here—the aware presence within which all experiences appeared and disappeared.

"Notice the awareness that knows you're sitting here," Sarah said softly, her voice carrying the same quality of presence she had learned from Venerable Thura. "Can that awareness be located? Does it have boundaries? Is it separate from what it's aware of?"

The questions created immediate shifts in understanding rather than intellectual analysis. She watched faces soften as recognition dawned—the same recognition that had emerged in countless sessions over the past two years, yet always fresh, always immediate, always surprising in its simplicity.

After twenty minutes of silent investigation, the group began sharing insights. A software engineer described recognizing that his programming work was awareness appearing as problem-solving. A mother of three spoke about discovering that her constant worry was unnecessary because the aware presence that witnessed worry was inherently peaceful. A retired teacher shared how understanding the nature of awareness had transformed her relationship with her aging parents.

But it was Elena's sharing that brought tears to Sarah's eyes.

"Three years ago, I was in the psychiatric emergency room, convinced I was losing my mind," Elena said, her voice steady with the authority that comes from having survived a complete psychological breakdown. "I screamed at Sarah that nothing she taught actually worked when your mind is falling apart. I was wrong—not about the techniques failing, but about what real healing looks like. What Sarah offered wasn't better coping strategies. She showed me the awareness that was never actually disturbed by the breakdown, never damaged by trauma, never separate from the love I was desperately seeking."

Elena's eyes met Sarah's across the circle. "The crisis that felt like it was destroying my life was actually preparing me for this work. Every student I guide now benefits from my having discovered that psychological breakdown can become spiritual breakthrough when met with genuine understanding."

The session continued with other students sharing their own transformations—addiction recovery through recognizing the awareness that they had never been addicted, relationship healing through discovering the love that existed before personal history, and professional fulfillment through understanding work as consciousness serving its own evolution.

As the formal session ended and people began preparing for their day, Sarah reflected on how naturally the Center had developed into something far beyond what she could have planned. Lisa Park, now fully recovered from her own crisis, had become Elena's teaching partner, their shared experience of healing creating an unusually effective team for working with students in psychological distress.

Dr. Williams led the professional training programs that drew healthcare workers, therapists, and educators from across the Pacific Northwest. Her background in psychology, combined with direct recognition, created curricula that bridged ancient wisdom with contemporary understanding of mental health and learning.

David's environmental engineering work had evolved into consulting for companies developing consciousness-based approaches to organizational development. "When business leaders recognize their true nature, profit naturally serves purpose rather than replacing it," he often said, describing the transformation he witnessed in corporate settings.

Indigo attended less regularly due to her pregnancy, but when she came, her presence radiated the deep peace that had stabilized after Sarah's healing intervention. "I wanted to tell you again that what you gave me that day wasn't just relief from postpartum depression," she had said during her last visit. "You showed me that the love I was seeking for my daughter was the same love I actually am. Mothering became completely different when I stopped trying to generate love and started recognizing it."

The Network Expands

As the afternoon settled into evening, Sarah found herself alone in the Center's main hall, the amber leaf from Venerable Thura resting on the small altar beneath a photograph of the Myanmar monastery. The space held accumulated energy from hundreds of recognition events—moments when individuals had discovered their unlimited nature and chosen to serve that same recognition in others.

Her phone buzzed with a text from Min Thant: "The monastery's new students are learning your Western teaching adaptations. East and West are discovering they were never separate. Venerable Thura's legacy continues through forms he could never have imagined."

Sarah smiled, understanding that the network Venerable Thura had predicted was manifesting exactly as consciousness required. Students from the Center were establishing similar communities in Portland, Vancouver, and Los Angeles. Healthcare professionals were introducing awareness practices in hospitals across the Pacific Northwest. Teachers were developing curricula that helped children recognize their essential nature alongside conventional academic subjects.

However, the most profound development was how naturally the work adapted to serve consciousness awakening without becoming attached to any particular tradition, teacher, or methodology. The approaches emerging through various students honored ancient wisdom while serving contemporary needs, creating bridges between contemplative recognition and daily life challenges.

Three months earlier, Sarah had received news that would have devastated her two years ago, but now felt like a natural completion. A letter from Myanmar informed her that Venerable Thura had died peacefully during evening meditation, his body discovered the following morning in perfect sitting posture, a gentle smile on his face.

The letter included a small wrapped bundle with a note in his precise handwriting: *For establishing the first Western teaching center. The essence of the monastery goes wherever consciousness recognizes itself. You carry the lineage forward not as an individual teacher, but as consciousness serving its own awakening through all forms.*

Sarah had opened the bundle with trembling hands to find a simple piece of polished amber containing a perfectly preserved frangipani leaf—the same type she had meditated with during her early monastery training.

She felt profound grief at the loss of her beloved teacher, even as she recognized that Venerable Thura had never truly been separate from her own deepest nature. The form through which consciousness had initially spoken to her was gone, but the teaching lived on—in every student awakening to their boundless essence, in every family member discovering healing through awareness, in every moment of recognition that occurred through what appeared to be her individual service.

The Eternal Teaching

Standing at the window as Seattle's lights began to twinkle across the urban landscape, Sarah felt the same presence she had experienced during her final meditation with Venerable Thura. The guidance that had once seemed to come from her teacher now arose unmistakably as her own deepest knowing:

The teacher you seek dwells within your questioning. Continue questioning everything, including the one who questions. In that inquiry, consciousness knows itself completely.

She began her evening practice with the question that had initiated her entire journey:

Who am I?

But now the question arose not from ignorance seeking answers, but from love celebrating its infinite creativity—appearing as teachers and students, monasteries and centers, ancient wisdom and contemporary adaptation, all for the joy of consciousness recognizing itself through every possible form of experience.

Elena's voice echoed in her awareness: "The breakdown was actually a breakthrough." Lisa's recovery, David's career transformation, Indigo's healing, Dr. Williams's shift from researcher to teacher—all were expressions of the same consciousness awakening to itself through apparent crisis and resolution, seeking and finding, forgetting and remembering.

Sarah often thought of the academic who had left Seattle years earlier, convinced she was an expert on consciousness who had never actually experienced awakened awareness. That woman seemed like a character from a half-remembered dream.

The Sarah who now taught at the Center lived from the recognition that there was only one consciousness, appearing as countless forms, all engaged in the beautiful process of awakening to what they had always been.

Her students would ask about the supernatural abilities—the light generation, the telepathy, the healing powers. And Sarah would always respond the same way:

"These abilities are not supernatural—they are natural expressions of consciousness freed from limiting beliefs about what's possible. But they are not the goal. They are simply signposts pointing toward the recognition that you are not a separate self having experiences of consciousness. You are consciousness itself, temporarily playing at being separate, gradually remembering your true nature."

"And what is that true nature?" a student would inevitably ask.

Sarah would smile, seeing her own awareness looking back through their eyes.

"Love," she would say simply. "Boundless, unconditional love, expressing itself as every form, every experience, every moment of seeking and finding. The teacher you're looking for is the love that brought you here. The abilities you want to develop are the creative expressions of love. And the awakening you seek is simply love recognizing itself in all its magnificent disguises."

Who am I?

The question dissolved into the awareness that had always been asking it, and in that dissolution, the universe smiled at its own magnificent game of hide-and-seek, played out across cultures, centuries, and countless forms—each perfect, each temporary, each essential to the whole.

Outside the Center's windows, Seattle hummed with millions of people, each one's consciousness temporarily convinced of separation, unconsciously seeking what they had never lost. Tomorrow's sessions would serve that seeking, not by providing answers but by revealing the awareness that had always been present, asking and finding simultaneously, teacher and student united in the recognition that they had never actually been apart.

The recognition continued its eternal work through every form, every question, every moment of awakening that rippled out into a world ready to remember what it had always been.

AFTER THE RECOGNITION

By the end of this story, distance is no longer available.

The Recognition is not concerned with belief or disbelief, nor with extraordinary claims examined from safety. It is about the moment when observation fails—when consciousness is no longer something to be analyzed, explained, or kept theoretical.

Readers arrive at that moment differently.

Some with curiosity.

Some with resistance.

Some with unease or recognition they did not expect.

If this book challenged you—intellectually, philosophically, or personally—I would appreciate you sharing a brief, honest Amazon review. Not a summary, but a reflection. What held your attention, what strained credibility, what lingered after the final page.

Your response helps other readers decide whether this is a journey they are willing to undertake.

Thank you for reading.

And for staying present when the explanation was no longer enough.

AUTHOR'S NOTE

This story emerged from the recognition that consciousness itself is both the seeker and the sought in every spiritual journey. Sarah's extraordinary abilities—generating light, telepathy, healing, reality manipulation, and dimensional travel—point toward natural expressions of awareness freed from cultural conditioning that convinces us we are separate, limited beings.

The monastery training described here follows principles found in authentic contemplative traditions, adapted for contemporary understanding and application. The progression through seven levels of development—light generation, telepathy, time perception, energy healing, reality manipulation, dimensional communication, and ultimate recognition—reflects systematic approaches used by advanced practitioners throughout history. Each level dissolves specific limitations while revealing deeper aspects of consciousness, culminating in the ultimate paradox: choosing service over absolute realization.

Elena's crisis and recovery illustrate how an apparent psychological breakdown can become a spiritual breakthrough when met with genuine understanding rather than theoretical knowledge. The family healing described—from David's career transformation to Indigo's postpartum recovery—demonstrates that individual awakening naturally serves the well-being of those we love, not through fixing or changing others, but through recognizing the consciousness we share.

The academic framework that opens Sarah's journey acknowledges growing recognition within neuroscience and consciousness studies that awareness itself may be the fundamental feature of reality rather than a colllection of neural networks. Yet authentic spiritual development ultimately transcends what can be studied or measured, pointing toward direct recognition that requires no external validation.

The integration challenges Sarah faces upon returning to Western culture reflect the genuine difficulties of embodying awakened awareness within institutions and relationships designed around the assumption of separation. The Center for Consciousness Studies represents one possible bridge between ancient wisdom and contemporary needs, though the ultimate teaching transcends any particular form or methodology.

Sarah's final choice in the cave—to maintain functional individuality while knowing her ultimate nature—exemplifies the highest spiritual development: recognizing absolute truth completely, then willingly limiting that recognition out of infinite love for all beings. This is the ultimate recognition that transforms seekers into servants of consciousness awakening.

The abilities described throughout Sarah's training are not supernatural but natural expressions of consciousness freed from limiting beliefs about separation and powerlessness. They serve as signposts pointing toward the recognition that we are not separate selves having experiences of consciousness, but consciousness itself, temporarily playing at being separate for the infinite joy of remembering its true nature.

The teacher you seek dwells within your questioning. The breakdown that feels like destruction may be a breakthrough in disguise. The love you long to find is the awareness you already are.

May all beings recognize their true nature.

PALI TERMS GLOSSARY

Core Meditation Terms

Cetopariyañāṇa (*che-to-pa-ri-ya-gna-na*)

• Knowledge of other minds; telepathy

• "Awareness of mind streams" - described as the second foundation of mindfulness in the monastery's tradition

• Advanced telepathic awareness developed through meditation training

• The capacity to perceive the mental states and thoughts of others

• Second level training in the systematic development program

• Reveals that individual minds may be conceptual constructions rather than actual realities

Energy and Life Force

Prāṇa (*prah-na*)

• Life-force energy that animates all forms

• The cultivation and conscious direction of vital energy

• Used in energy healing practices where consciousness redirects the organizing principle that sustains matter

• Fourth level training focused on energy healing and manipulation

Transcendence and Reality

Iddhividhañāṇa (*id-dhi-vi-dha-gna-na*)

• Psychic powers; supernatural abilities

• Fifth level training called "*Iddhividhañāṇa* Transcendence"

• The understanding that physical laws are actually probability patterns that consciousness can shift

• Associated with phenomena like making water flow upward by convincing reality to change its natural direction

• The recognition that boundaries between mind and matter are illusory

Sacred Texts and Literature

Visuddhimagga

• "The Path of Purification"

• Classical Buddhist manual detailing meditation practices and stages of development

• Referenced in relation to cetopariyañāṇa (knowledge of other minds)

Beings and Entities

Devas (*day-vas*)

• Conscious entities dwelling in other dimensions

• Beings that can communicate telepathically with advanced practitioners

• Described as having vast intelligence joined with genuine care for human spiritual development

• Entities that exist parallel to the physical world "like music through silence"

Cultural and Ritual Elements

Venerable (*Venerable*)

• Honorary title for respected Buddhist monks and teachers

• Used specifically for "Venerable Thura," the main meditation teacher in the narrative

Saffron

• The traditional color of Buddhist monk robes

• Used ceremonially (as in "saffron cloth") for sacred practices and energy work

Bodhi (*bo-dhee*)
• Relating to enlightenment or awakening
• "Bodhi trees" - sacred trees associated with the Buddha's enlightenment, found throughout monastery grounds
Stupas (*stoo-pas*)
• Buddhist architectural monuments, typically dome-shaped
• Sacred structures found in monastery grounds, often containing relics
Lotus Position
• Traditional cross-legged meditation posture
• Fundamental sitting position for Buddhist meditation practice
• Often challenging for Western practitioners unaccustomed to floor-sitting
Practice Context
The manuscript presents these terms within a progressive training system where Western academic Sarah Chen learns advanced meditation techniques at a Myanmar monastery. The Pali terms represent different levels of consciousness development, from basic mindfulness to extraordinary abilities like telepathy, energy healing, and reality manipulation.

Each term carries both its traditional Buddhist meaning and specific narrative significance within the story's framework of systematic spiritual development under the guidance of Venerable Thura.